WRECKERS' BAY

BLACKIE & SON LIMITED
66 Chandos Place, LONDON
17 Stanhope Street, GLASGOW

BLACKIE & SON (INDIA) LIMITED
103/5 Fort Street, BOMBAY

BLACKIE & SON (CANADA) LIMITED
TORONTO

E 770

EAGER HANDS REACHED OUT TO HIM

Page 71

Frontispiece

WRECKERS' BAY

BY

PERCY WOODCOCK

Frontispiece by Dudley Tennant

BLACKIE & SON LIMITED
LONDON AND GLASGOW

BOOK,
PRODUCTION
WAR ECONOMY
STANDARD

Printed in Great Britain by Blackie & Son, Ltd., Glasgow

Contents

WRECKERS' BAY

CHAPTER I

The First Day of the Holidays

" What are you two boys going to do with yourselves to-day?"

Major Bamford, the speaker, a jovial man of fifty, lowered his copy of the *Morning Post* and looked from his son, Anthony, to Jack Forster, who were engaged in disposing of their final helping of buttered toast and marmalade.

They exchanged glances.

" I don't know, Dad. We haven't decided, but we'll find something."

" I expect you will," said his father, smiling. " I have to go over to Dovermouth to-day. I'm on the bench and, from what the inspector tells me, there's a troublesome case down for hearing that will probably take some time, so, as I may not be back to lunch, don't wait for me."

Major Bamford rose.

" You must get Tony to show you round," he said, laying his hand in kindly fashion on Jack's shoulder as he passed.

" Yes, sir," replied Jack cheerfully, with his mouth full.

" No need to worry about how we'll amuse ourselves," said Tony as the door closed. " It's jolly enough just to be able to do as we like for a change. No call-overs, no lessons, no masters, no drills, no bells—except for meals," he added, with a laugh. " There's a big bell on the side of the house and they ring it a quarter of an hour before meal times. We can hear it from the grounds."

Tony and Jack were clad in flannels and, as their blazers and badges showed, went to the same school. They had, in fact, just completed their first term at St. Aldham's, where they had met as the only new boys in their form, and the forced comradeship of settling down as strangers in strange surroundings had quickly ripened into a genuine and close friendship. Jack's parents were in India, so, to their mutual delight, it had been arranged that he should spend his holidays in Tony's home.

Tony was an only child and, his mother having died some years before, lived alone with his father in Barlash Hall, which was low and long and built of grey stone, with a roof composed of great slabs of the same material. The house stood in its own grounds and, from its windows, looked out across lawns and shrubberies down a valley to where the cottages of the village of Barlash clustered on the edge of the little cove. Beyond was a far-away glimpse of the open sea.

"Finished?" asked Tony, a few moments later. "Come on, then. Let's go down to the cove."

Through the open French windows they stepped out on to the lawn and, passing through the shrubbery, climbed a wire fence to take a short cut to the village.

In the little street, with its quaint irregular cottages, "all shapes and sizes" as Jack put it, their progress was slower, for Tony had to stop to answer the greetings of the villagers. As they neared a little shop, half sweetshop, half pastrycook's, a face could be seen peering through the diamond panes of the bow window and, as they drew nearer, a hand knocked vigorously on the glass.

"It's no good," said Tony, with a sheepish look at Jack. "Old Anne has seen me. We'll have to go in."

They entered the shop and stood on the sanded stone floor while a flood of greeting poured over the wood-topped counter from a little old woman in a spotless white cap and apron, and with the roundest, pinkest, cheeriest face Jack had ever seen.

"There you are, Master Tony. I heard you'd come home, so I was keeping a lookout for you, for I knew you'd be down to have a look at the boats the very first thing. What a boy you are for the water, to be sure! Here, let me look at you." She moved round the counter. "Yes, you've grown again, surely. Bigger than ever you are and growing more like your dear father every day. I minds the time well enough when he was just such another as you. Let me see. How old are you? Your birthday is to-morrow, I know. Fourteen you'll be, isn't it? Bless me, how the time do fly."

So the good old dame rattled on while Tony, with a covert wink at Jack, waited for the flood to run dry.

"Well, well," she said at last. "I suppose you'll be wanting to be off. You'll have lots of things you'll be wanting to be doing without wasting your time with an old body like me. Here, take this, Master Tony, and here's one for you too, Master—Jack, is it? And now don't get doing nothing venturesome. Your father was a one for that. Always in some mischief or other."

At length the boys found themselves back in the road, the richer by a packet of chocolate apiece.

"What a funny old girl," commented Jack, as he broke his packet open. "But how jolly."

"Yes," agreed Tony. "She is funny, isn't she? She was father's nurse when he was a baby and her daughter was mine, so she always makes a fearful fuss. She seems to think she owns us, but she's a dear old thing really and so is her husband. He's a fisherman. Let's go and see what Bill Pascoe, the boatbuilder, is doing."

Munching steadily, they entered the yard. It was an interesting place. The ground, littered with untidy piles of timber, a heap of rusty chain, a broken capstan and other maritime oddments, sloped steadily to the water. A battered figurehead, a relic of some long-deceased vessel, stood derelict in one corner, while three sheds of varying sizes looked in the last stages of dilapidation. A small box-like structure with a corrugated-iron roof, standing just inside the gate, was in better repair, and bore the legend " Office " roughly painted on a piece of wood above a slit for letters in the door.

Bill Pascoe and his two sons were busily engaged in putting new bolts in the iron keel of a fishing boat which they had " struck over " on her side. Bill greeted the boys with a cheery shout and then continued his work, striking shrewd blows at the protruding bolt with a heavy maul. Tony and Jack stood by for a time watching.

" Have you built anything new lately?" asked Tony, during a pause in the operations.

" There's a new boat in that shed there," said Tom, one of the sons.

" Oh, do let us see her!" cried Tony in an eager voice.

Bill gave his son a glance of annoyance.

" Well," he said, " she's in that there shed all right, but Tom here was doing a job to her last evening and he have gone and mislaid the key."

" Oh!" cried Tony.

" I expects it'll turn up," said Bill. " If it don't, we'll just have to break in, that's all, but we may as well wait awhile because we've got this job on hand and no call to go in there and 'tis no good to smash up a good door needless."

"I should like to have seen her," said Tony in a disappointed voice.

"You'll see her all right by and by, Master Tony," said Tom Pascoe cheerfully. "I expect I'll find the key come to-morrow and you'll be down again, I reckon."

The work was resumed and, after watching for a little while longer, the boys moved on.

"Let's go up on the cliff by the Watch House," suggested Tony.

"Anywhere you like," agreed Jack. "You know what there is to see better than I do."

They finished the last of their chocolate as they climbed the steep hillside and, emerging suddenly at the top of the turf-clad slope, found themselves on the edge of a precipitous cliff.

It was a lovely view. To the west the rocky coast showed bold and rugged, to end in a grim headland nearly two miles away. To the east the coast receded into a deep bay, in which the little cove of Barlash was situated. Farther on the lower shores by Dovermouth were dimly visible in the haze.

It was a beautiful summer's day with scarcely a cloud in the sky, and the calm water lay smooth and unruffled save for the fringe of white where the almost imperceptible swell curled over and broke on the sandy beach at the cliff foot, nearly two hundred feet below.

"What a queer-looking steamer!" said Jack, pointing to a vessel on the horizon. "What is she? Is she a warship?"

" I can't make her out at all," said Tony. " She looks more like an oil tanker to me, but watch, she seems to be changing, though, of course, that can't be possible. Is she a sailing vessel? She looks to have —one, two, three, four—I believe she's a four-masted barque."

" I don't think she's a sailing vessel," said Jack. " I could swear she had two funnels just now."

" It's awfully queer," said Tony. " I've never seen anything like it. I know. Come on to the Watch House. I expect Tom Wallis will be there. He'll have a telescope and will let us have a look."

The Watch House was barely a hundred yards away. It was a little white-washed stone hut, with a slate roof, surrounded by a wire fence. A white-painted flagstaff, from the yard of which floated a white ensign, stood in one corner of the enclosure.

Tony opened the iron gate and advanced up the path to the half-open door.

" Come in, come in!" cried a man's voice heartily, as they reached the threshold. " I saw you along the cliff, so I thought you'd be giving me a call before long."

Thus invited, Tony pushed the door open, and the boys entered. Jack looked round him with interest. The interior of the hut was barely ten feet square, but was spick and span, and the boarded floor showed signs of frequent scrubbings. A table, which evidently served also as a desk, stood against one wall. The stove and scuttle, empty now, shone brightly of black-lead and gave promise of a cheery warmth when the winter gales howled outside. Sundry notices and instructions for reviving the apparently drowned were pinned to the walls, though one side was entirely taken up with a case like an overgrown letter-rack, but, instead of correspondence, each little lettered pigeon-hole was filled with a rolled-up ball of bunting.

The seaward side of the hut held a wide window, in which stood an enormous telescope, while a man, evidently Tom Wallis, clad in a double-breasted suit of rough blue serge, stood beside it.

" Holidays started again?" he cried in cheery welcome. " How long is it this time? Seven weeks and four days. Come, that's a good spell, sure enough. What will you find to do with yourself all that long time? Who's your friend?"

Tony introduced Jack, who manfully tried not to wince as his hand was crushed in the coast watcher's huge fist.

" What's that funny vessel out there?" asked Tony.

" Take a look at her," said Tom Wallis, making way for them at the telescope. The boys looked in turn, each lifting a puzzled face from the instrument.

Tom laughed at their expressions.

" Can't make her out, can you?" he asked. " No more could I if I saw her now, as you have done, but I saw her before the fog came on. She's a white steam yacht. It's the fog making her look queer. She's just on the edge of it and it makes her loom up all out of shape. There, it's swallowed her up. You can't see her at all now."

It was as he said. The vessel had entirely disappeared.

" It's funny I didn't notice the fog," said Tony.

" That is because it is so calm. The sea and the sky near the horizon are the same colour as the fog and you couldn't see where one began and the other ended. It's coming closer now. There, you can see the edge of the bank."

He put his eye to the glass and stared intently at a fishing boat which, with its motor running, was approaching from the direction of the distant yacht.

" What is it, Tom?" asked Tony.

" Only young Sam Tonkin in his fishing boat."

" Do let me see."

Young Sam Tonkin was old Anne's grandson and five years Tony's senior. His father had been in the Royal Naval Reserve and, called to the colours on the outbreak of the Great War, had lost his life when the cruiser in which he was serving had been sunk by the torpedo of a submarine. His mother was ill at the time and never recovered from the shock of hearing of the death of her husband, so the orphaned boy had been brought up by his grandparents, old Sam and Anne Tonkin. Anne Tonkin's acquaintance we have already made in the sweetshop.

Tony had often been taken out fishing in the holidays by old Sam Tonkin and, as his grandson usually went too, the boys had seen a good deal of each other and, despite the difference in their ages and their social position, a genuine friendship had grown up between the two. Now Sam had grown into a big strong youth and, with his grandfather growing older and more and more crippled with rheumatism, had come almost to man's estate, taking the boat out alone as often as not. Tony, in his last holidays, had several times gone out with him, leaving the old man on shore, and had helped Sam haul his crabpots and long lines, so he stared hard at his friend.

" How funny," he commented. " Sam seems to be looking straight up here."

" Yes," said Tom, in a peculiar tone. " There's more than one would like to see this telescope done away with. Hullo, here comes the fog."

A cold breath was in the air and the white fog bank came rolling across the sea. A few moments later, Sam, his boat and, indeed, the very sea itself were hidden, and wisps of the grey vapour rolled up the cliff face and over the edge of the down, shrouding everything in a dim whiteness.

Tom Wallis withdrew the telescope from the window and closed it.

" No more use for this now," he said. " This is just the weather for the job, isn't it?"

" Just the weather for what job?" asked Tony, puzzled by the man's manner.

Tom looked at him for a moment as though about to say more, then he changed the subject.

" Ever seen the International Code of signals?" he

asked, turning to Jack, and he went on to explain the intricacies of the signal book; how each flag represented a letter of the alphabet and how combinations of the flags, or letters, made up whole sentences. Only the previous week, he told them, a little French schooner had been standing too close in to the dreaded rocks of the Wreckers' reef in a strong wind. He had seen her and had watched her approach with a growing anxiety; then, seeing she made no sign of going about, he had seized the two flags " J D ", which, as he showed by reference to the huge leather-bound book, mean " You are standing into danger ", and had run them up on the flagstaff. The fluttering bunting had caught the steersman's eye, and a few moments later the little schooner had put about and stood out to sea and safety again just in time.

The boys stayed chatting with their friend for nearly an hour.

" What an interesting chap!" commented Jack, as he and Tony left the hut.

" Yes," agreed Tony thoughtfully. " But did you notice he nearly told us something and then switched off on to telling you about the signals? I wonder what it was. I nearly asked him, but I didn't quite like to."

" I didn't notice," said Jack. " I was so jolly interested in what he was saying, I didn't notice anything else. Where are we going now?"

" Let's go down to the beach. There's a path down the cliff about half a mile away. It's steep and a bit of a scramble, but come on."

He started at a jog trot and Jack joined him.

" I say, this fog is getting awfully thick. Sure you know the way?"

" Of course," laughed Tony. " Anyway, we've only got to follow the cliff edge and we can't possibly miss it."

The fog was indeed thick. Little beads of moisture formed on their clothing, which felt wet to the touch when they passed a hand over it, and the breath came from their lips like smoke.

" Hullo!" said Jack. " Is that a man?"

A dark shape loomed in the mist ahead. The boys approached. It was a man, clad in a fisherman's thick blue guernsey, rough trousers and heavy sea boots. He was standing at the edge of the down, where a narrow track branched off from the path and led to the beach below. Intently staring seaward, he had not heard the boys approach, their footfalls being muffled on the damp ground.

" Hullo!" cried Tony. " What are you looking at?"

Old Sam Tonkin, for it was he, turned with a start.

" Why, Master Tony, how are ye, boy? I'm right glad to see ye home again." He seized Tony's hand in one of his and, laying the other on the boy's shoulder, looked him keenly over. " You're looking fine, sure enough.

" And where be you off to this mucky weather?" he asked, after greeting Jack.

" Down to the beach," said Tony.

The old man hesitated.

" I wouldn't now, if I was you. 'Tis cold and dampish down there with this nasty old fog about. I should get back along home. You'll maybe find that 'tis all sunshiny across the valley. This here is only sea fog and I don't reckon it do go far inland."

" It won't hurt us, Sam," protested Tony. " It's nothing. Besides, I want to show Jack the caves."

The old man shook his head.

" Not this morning, I wouldn't go, Master Tony. 'Twill be all damp and drippy in the caves."

" It always is!" cried Tony, laughing. " Come on, Jack."

At that moment a low whistle sounded from below. It was repeated. Old Sam caught Tony by the arm.

" Now don't go down to the beach this morning. Get along back home like a good boy."

Tony stared in open-mouthed astonishment.

" I asks you to go back along home," reiterated the old man earnestly. " Will ye do it now, please."

" Oh, all right, Sam," said Tony, impressed by his manner. " If you're so set on it, but why?"

" Now that I can't tell 'ee," said the old man, loosing the boy's arm, " only run along, now do. The cliffs ain't healthy with this fog about."

" I can't understand Sam," said Tony, as they walked away and the old man's figure was once more lost in the fog. " It's all nonsense about sea fog hurting anyone. I've been out in it lots of times and none the worse. There's something funny going on that I——"

He stopped dead as the double whistle sounded again faintly behind them.

" It certainly seems funny," agreed Jack. " It sounds as though it were a signal."

" I'm sure it is," said Tony definitely.

They climbed a rough stone wall and crossed a field, taking a short cut to the road which was their nearest way back to Barlash Hall. Climbing the high earth bank, which formed the hedge on the farther side, they dropped into the road almost on the top of a man who stood at the corner peering out across the down. He leapt round as he heard them and one hand slipped behind him. The three faced each other for a moment in silence, then the man gave a short laugh.

" You boys startled me," he said, and turned his back on them to resume his stare out towards the invisible sea.

Forty yards away, farther down the lane, a big saloon car was standing, drawn close to the bank. A woman sat at the wheel. She glanced at them sharply as they approached and then turned her head away and kept her face averted so that they could not see her features.

" What a lovely car! Did you see, it was a Sunbeam?" said Jack, as they drew out of earshot.

" Yes," agreed Tony absently.

" A penny for them," challenged Jack, after they had walked for fifty yards in silence.

" Well," said Tony, frowning, " it seems to me there's something very funny going on. It may be all bilge and just coincidence, of course, but just think what's happened to us this morning. Here's a strange car in the road. I wouldn't think much of that, but the man was standing watching for something, or seemed to be."

" They may be just visitors," suggested Jack. " I didn't notice, but they may have had luggage with them in the back of the car."

" They may," agreed Tony doubtfully. " But why wouldn't old Sam let us go down to the beach? And what about the whistling? We heard it. Twice. It may not have been a signal, but it sounded jolly like it. And then there was Tom Wallis. He nearly said something to us and then changed his mind."

" Yes," agreed Jack chaffingly. " And there was that locked shed at the boatbuilder's. Perhaps there was something hidden in that, too."

Tony stopped dead, and it was obvious that his friend's chaffing remark struck him as serious.

" There is something funny going on," he said decisively. " Come on, it must be nearly lunch time. I shall tell Dad about it and ask him what he thinks."

But Major Bamford, as he had expected, was unable to get back to lunch and, in the afternoon, the boys played an exciting game of cricket, commandeering the services of the gardener, David Ellis, who had played for his county as a fast bowler in his day and, though getting old and stiff, could still send down a ball with something of his old cunning in it even if the sting of the speed had gone. The consequence was that, by the time the Major came home, the affairs of the morning had faded in Tony's mind and, in the general conversation, Tony forgot to mention his suspicions. It was not until the boys were tumbling into bed that Jack remembered and reminded him.

" You never told your father about what happened this morning," he said.

" No more I did. I forgot all about it," confessed Tony. " Never mind, I'll ask him at breakfast in the morning."

CHAPTER II

Tony's Birthday

" Many happy returns." Jack raised a tousled head from the pillow and grinned across at his chum.

" Thanks," came the reply, muffled by the bed-clothes. Tony lay still for a minute and then, rolling over, sat up.

" What sort of a day is it?" he asked, rubbing his eyes sleepily.

" Topping. I can see the sky all blue. Not a cloud in sight."

At that moment a bell sounded.

" Turn out," said Tony. " Breakfast will be on in a jiff."

Twenty minutes later they entered the breakfast-room. Tony looked round eagerly. Nothing by his plate, or by his chair. Had his father forgotten? He had never done so before, but he had not mentioned his birthday yesterday and usually there was a lovely surprise waiting for him. His spirits fell a little. At that moment his father entered.

" Morning, boys. Many happy returns, Tony. Are you looking round for your present? I'm afraid you won't see it here, but I haven't forgotten you."

" What is it, Dad?"

" Never you mind, young man, you eat your breakfast," he went on banteringly. " You'll learn all in good time."

So Tony had to possess his soul with what patience he could muster till the meal was eaten. Even then his curiosity was not immediately satisfied.

" Don't go away, boys," said the Major, as he rose. " I want you to walk down to the village with me, but I have a letter to write first."

An hour later the three of them were walking down the village street and again were the victims of old Anne Tonkin's watchfulness. As they drew near her shop she appeared in the doorway, beckoning them within, and again the boys left the richer by packets of chocolate, while Jack was amused and surprised to notice that the old dame addressed his friend's father as " Master Anthony ".

Major Bamford lagged behind as they left the shop and slipped something that rustled into the old woman's hand.

" Thank you kindly, Master Anthony," said Mrs. Tonkin, her eyes filling with tears. " You've been that kind to me all my life, you have. And I can't say but what we needs it, for the fishing be that bad, there's little enough money in the village. Young Sam do get impatient, that he do. He do say the fishing be finished."

" Tell him to have patience," said the Major as he took his leave.

"Hullo!" he said, as they reached the bottom of the street. "What has Pascoe got the flags up for? Let's go to see."

Pascoe's yard was indeed a cheering sight. A huge red ensign fluttered from the top of the mast of the fishing boat hauled up on the slip and now upright on her keel once more, and three strings of flags stretched from her masthead in different directions across the yard, giving it a festive appearance.

"It must be some special occasion," said the Major. "Perhaps he is going to launch a new boat."

"Yes, that will be it!" cried Tony. "He said there was a new boat in his big shed yesterday, but he'd mislaid the key so we never saw her. Do let's go and watch."

The missing key had evidently been found, for the doors of the big shed were gaping wide, and launching ways, made of planks, had been laid to the water.

"Ah, there you are, sir," said the boatbuilder. "Just in time. Tide's on the turn. Many happy returns, Master Tony. We've found the key, you see."

As they reached the open end of the shed and were able to look inside, Tony gave a gasp. In the shed, resplendent in new paint and varnish, lay a boat and on her stern hung a board bearing the words:

TONY

MANY HAPPY RETURNS

" Oh, Dad, is this my present?"

His father nodded, smiling.

Tony could scarcely trust himself to speak. He had always longed for a boat of his own, but the secret had been well kept and he had no idea that this lovely surprise was coming. He looked at the smiling faces round him and then gave his father's arm a squeeze of gratitude.

" Why, how jolly!" cried Jack, noticing the shining little gun-metal propeller. " She's got a motor."

" Yes," said the boatbuilder. " She's like the fisher-men. She can either sail or motor."

They crowded round her, critically examining her. She was indeed a boat to gladden the heart of any boy who loved the sea. Seventeen feet long, six feet wide, drawing nearly three feet of water and with a heavy lead keel bolted on outside to keep her from capsizing, she was a safe, wholesome type of craft, very similar, as the boatbuilder said, to the boats owned by the local fishermen, but built of better materials and beautifully finished. She was " half decked ", which means that the deck extended from the bows to behind the mast, forming a little " cuddy " into which the boys could just squeeze and squat down; then there was a foot or so of deck right aft across the stern, and the " water-ways ", or side decks, connected the two, leaving a large, oval-shaped, open " well ", in which the crew could sit and in the middle of which was a little two-cylinder motor under a neat teakwood casing.

She was to be yawl rigged with staysail, mainsail,

and a little mizzen on its own mast aft, but, being in the shed, the masts and sails were not in place, and lay in a fascinating heap on the long bench which ran along the side of the building.

Tony took it all in with a growing wonder. He had dreamed of such a boat, but had never believed he would actually own one, not like this and for his very own. Not for years and years anyway. He could hardly credit his good fortune. Jack was no whit less excited. Together they fingered this and that, while Major Bamford and the boatbuilder watched with understanding sympathy and exchanged glances of mutual congratulation.

" Oh, Dad, she's lovely!" cried Tony at length.

" I'm glad you like her," said his father quietly.

" What are you going to call her?" asked the boatbuilder. " We must launch her soon, if she's to go afloat this tide, and she ought to be christened first."

" *Spray!*" cried Tony promptly. His " dream ship " had always borne that name.

" And who is going to christen her?"

" Well, now, I must confess I never thought of that," said Major Bamford. " I've brought a bottle of wine, but I never thought about who should do the actual christening."

" What's all the excitement?" said a voice behind them, and the Major turned to see the Rev. Graham Temple, the vicar, behind him.

" Good morning, Major; morning, Pascoe; morning everybody," said that gentleman. " I saw the decorations, so I came in to find what it was all about."

"You're the very man we want!" cried the Major.
"Tony's boat is just going to be launched and we want
someone to christen her."

"Of course, I'm afraid I'd forgotten. Many happy
returns, Tony, and may you have the best of years,
but, surely, Major, you ought to have a lady to do the
christening."

"That's just what we haven't got, vicar," said Major
Bamford, laughing.

"May I suggest my wife, then," said the vicar.
"She's in the grocer's over the road and I'm sure she
will be only too glad to take part in the ceremony.
Shall I fetch her?"

"Do, by all means," said the Major heartily.

With the boatbuilder and his men on either side
of her, the new boat was carefully slid down the ways
until she was half out of the shed. Then, taking the
bottle of wine from Major Bamford, Tom Pascoe
suspended it from the bow of the boat by a stout
cord.

"There, I reckon that will do," said the boatbuilder. "Now, m'm," he added, turning to Mrs.
Temple, who had arrived while the operation was in
progress and, in answer to Major Bamford's request,
had readily agreed to perform the christening ceremony.
"See you give the bottle a good hard slam against the
bow; it's bad luck for the ship if it don't break."

"In that case," said Mrs. Temple, smiling, "I
must do my best."

She took the bottle in her hand, while Major Bamford, her husband, Tony, Jack, the boatbuilder and his men formed a semicircular group around her.

"I christen you *Spray*, and may you be a happy ship!" cried Mrs. Temple in loud, clear tones.

She swung the bottle wide and, after a tense moment of suspense, it crashed into pieces against the bow and the sparkling wine ran down the new paint.

The boatbuilder breathed a sigh of relief.

"Knock that dog out, Tom. Give her a start. All together, boys, heave! There she goes!"

"There she goes!" echoed Tom and his brother workmen, raising the old, old cry of the shipbuilders as they see the work of their hands start on her first journey down the ways to her native element.

The *Spray*, for such we must now call her, slid stern foremost down the well-greased planking, gathering speed as she went. Her keel broke the surface, she sank lower and lower and, while the bow was still high in the air, her flat transom stern plunged deep so that the water boiled up level with the taffrail, and for one horrified moment the boys thought she was going to plunge straight to the bottom, then suddenly she was afloat and riding serenely on an even keel, swaying and curtsying before she came to rest.

"Now!" cried the boatbuilder, snatching off his battered sawdust-covered hat, "all together—hip—hip—hip——"

The three cheers rose heartily on the summer air.

"You don't generally launch a boat as small as the

Spray in such an impressive fashion, do you?" asked the Major, in a quiet aside to Mr. Pascoe.

"Well, no, sir," replied that worthy, a trifle sheepishly; "but it wasn't much trouble and I thought, as it's a special occasion, it would please the boy."

"It has certainly done that," said the Major, with a glance at Tony, who, with Jack beside him, stood at the water's edge, gazing with all his eyes at his new possession. "Thank you very much."

"Haul her in!" cried the boatbuilder, practical once more. "We'll put her alongside the wharf," he explained to the Major, "then we can step the masts, bend sails and finish her off."

"We may stay to help, mayn't we, Dad?" cried Tony, hearing the words.

"Of course," agreed his father readily. "I don't suppose I shall see much of you to-day, but don't forget to come home to lunch at one o'clock."

His final words fell on deaf ears. The boys were already on the edge of the wharf, assisting to moor the *Spray* alongside.

"Don't worry, sir," said Mr. Pascoe, laughing, "I'll send them home when we knocks off for the dinner hour at half-past twelve."

So, with a final amused look at his son and with the knowledge that his birthday present had been an unqualified success, Major Bamford strolled out of the yard in company with Mr. and Mrs. Temple.

.   .   .   .

Tony and Jack spent a strenuous but wonderfully

happy day, and when they finally tore themselves away from the *Spray* her masts were " stepped ", her rigging was " set up ", her running gear " rove off " and her sails " bent ". Everything aboard her was, as the boatbuilder expressed it, quoting the old sea saying, " shipshape and Bristol fashion ". The *Spray* was indeed " ready for sea " and they could look forward to a trial sail on the morrow.

" I say," said Jack, pushing back the clothes, a few moments after tumbling into bed that night, and looking across the room at his chum with a mischievous twinkle in his eye, " what about those funny happenings yesterday? The whistles and the motor-car and the mystery of the locked shed—with a new boat inside?"

" Oh, shut up," said Tony, laughing happily.

CHAPTER III

The Trial Trip of the New Boat

The boys were " up with the lark " the next morning, all anxiety to get down to the *Spray*, and chafed at having to wait for breakfast.

" It's no good being in such a hurry," said Major Bamford. " The *Spray* won't run away and, in any case, there's no wind, so you cannot possibly sail."

" But we can try the motor, sir," said Jack, who was no less eager than Tony.

" Yes, Dad, of course we can!" cried Tony. " So it doesn't matter a bit if there is no wind."

" Oh, get along with you," said the Major, laughing. " However, there goes the gong, so come along in to breakfast."

The boys hurried through the meal; they would, indeed, have scamped it altogether had not the Major insisted on their eating " something ", as he called it, but at last they satisfied him and got his permission to go. They raced down the valley and through the village at their top speed and arrived at the boat-builder's panting and out of breath.

" Hullo!" cried Mr. Pascoe, on catching sight of them. " Be the French landed, or is the house on fire? It's all right, Master Tony," he went on, laughing, " the *Spray* is on her moorings, safe and sound, and Tom be ready to take you for the trial trip. There's no wind yet, but," with a weatherwise look at the glorious blue sky, " I reckon there'll be a nice little southerly breeze by and by. Tom!"

In answer to his stentorian hail, his son appeared from one of the sheds. Nodding a cheerful greeting to the boys, he led the way to a rowing boat and a few minutes later the boys were aboard the *Spray*, which lay on her moorings in the little cove.

There was, indeed, not a breath of wind, but Tom agreed with his father's verdict as to the coming of the " nice little breeze by and by " and suggested that they should set the sails before leaving the moorings, then they could start under power and would be all ready for the wind when it arrived.

Jack learned many things while the *Spray* was being got ready—how new sails must be treated gently and must not be pulled out too tightly on the " gaff " and " boom ", or there was grave risk of spoiling the shape and so ruining the sails for life; that " sheets " are not sails, as he had thought, but ropes which pull the sails in and out to " trim " them to the best advantage to catch the wind, and that " halyards " are other ropes by which the sails are hoisted and lowered.

The little three-cornered " leg of mutton " mizzen was set first on its diminutive mast at the stern, then the jib was hoisted. The latter sail was fitted with Wykeham Martin furling gear, which enabled it to be rolled up, when hoisted, by pulling on a line and unrolled again by a pull on its sheet.

"How easy!" commented Tony, who had not seen one of these fittings before.

"Yes," agreed Tom Pascoe, "it saves a lot of trouble and is very handy, as you'll find when you come to pick up the moorings. You can roll the sail up quick and get it out of the way and then take it down when it suits you."

The mainsail was also hoisted. When properly "set", the spar on its foot, called the "boom", just comfortably cleared their heads as they sat in the cockpit, but, when they stood up, they found they were liable to get a knock on the head if they did not look out.

"Now," said Tom, when these preparations were completed, "let's have a look at the engine."

Slipping a couple of catches, he lifted the lid of the casing and revealed the engine, a fascinating mass of bright green paint and shining brasswork, and for the next few minutes explained its peculiarities.

The motor, of course, worked like any other motor, but, unlike that of a car, had no varying speed gears, but just a simple "ahead" and "astern" position, in addition to the neutral, the speed of the vessel being controlled by the throttle and spark levers. Having started and run the engine himself for a few moments, Tom stopped it again.

"Now," he said to Tony, "you had better try your hand at starting it."

Nothing loth, Tony took the priming can and opened the priming cocks on the heads of the cylinders. Then he squirted petrol into the cylinders.

"Not too much," warned Tom. "If you over-prime, you'll get too rich a mixture and she may not start. A few drops are enough."

The engine was not fitted with a self-starter, so had to be turned by hand, but Major Bamford had thought of this and had had an impulse starter fitted to the magneto, which caused a fierce spark even when the handle was pulled over slowly, so it was possible for a person of little physical strength to start the engine.

"What about the ignition?" warned Tom, as Tony laid hold of the starting handle. "Is it retarded?"

Tony inspected the lever, pushing it back to make sure.

"Always watch that," said his mentor. "You may get a backfire else, and that may mean a sprained wrist, if no worse."

Rather gingerly Tony pulled the lever over. The motor remained impassive.

"Try again," said Tom.

Tony tried again. This time the handle was harder to turn, and he had to change his position and stand squarely to his task.

"You've got the compression this time," laughed Tom.

Exerting his strength, Tony pulled the handle over and, to his great delight, the motor started, running with a gentle purr.

" Jolly good!" cried Jack, who had been an interested spectator. " That's fine."

" Now you try," said Tom Pascoe, turning to him, after Tony had worked the controls for a few minutes.

Tony stopped the engine and Jack took his place, to find that he could start it as easily as Tony had done. They each had second attempts, which were as successful as their firsts.

" I think you've mastered that all right," said Tom Pascoe. " One's apt to forget things at first, so I've noted down those you've got to remember. If you look this over before you begin, you ought not to go far wrong."

As he spoke, he drew from his jacket pocket a square piece of three-ply wood on which he had printed, evidently with a carpenter's broad pencil, the following:

> Turn on the petrol.
> Turn on the water cock.
> Put lever into neutral.
> Retard the spark.
> Adjust the throttle.
> Prime the cylinders.
> Swing her.

" Oh, thanks, Tom!" cried Tony, when he and Jack had read these simply worded yet explicit instructions. " This is just what we want."

" Now," said Tom, " I'll slip the moorings. Who is going to be skipper and who engineer?"

The boys looked at one another.

" She's your boat, so you ought to be skipper," said Jack.

" All right," said Tony, taking the tiller. " You start the engine."

" All gone!" called Tom, throwing the buoy overboard when the motor had resumed its purring.

" Go ahead," ordered Tony.

Jack pushed in the clutch and opened the throttle. The *Spray* began to forge ahead.

" Watch the buoy," warned Tom. " I've thrown it well clear and you must remember to do that every time. If you drop it underfoot, you may steam right over it, and then, as likely as not, it'll catch the rope in the propeller and you'll have a fine old mess up."

For the next hour the boys had a thrilling time. Under the steady thrust of the propeller, the *Spray* developed a good turn of speed, estimated by Tom Pascoe at " nigh on six knots ", and the foaming waves, curling away from the bows with a steady hiss, and the bubble-filled wake were a joy to watch.

" I'm a passenger," said Tom Pascoe at last, pulling out a pouch of tobacco and filling his pipe. " That crabpot over there is the buoy on the moorings. I'm not here. You two are by yourselves. Let's see what sort of a fist you make of picking it up."

The boys accepted the challenge. Tony took the tiller and Jack stood by the engine controls. As they drew near the buoy, Tony gave the order to slow down. Jack closed the throttle a little.

" Stop her."

Jack threw out the clutch and throttled right down as the engine raced. The *Spray* carried her way over the calm water in a fashion that astonished the boys, and was still travelling at a good speed when the little bundle of corks was almost under the bow.

" Go astern!" cried Tony. " Full speed astern," he added a moment later.

Jack pulled the clutch into the necessary position and again opened the throttle. The water boiled under the stern and the *Spray* gradually lost speed and at last came to a standstill, but, as she stopped, her bow turned away from the cork float so that Tony, when he ran forward to pick it up, was unable to reach it. He turned such a surprised and puzzled face on Tom that that worthy burst into good-humoured laughter.

" Never mind, Master Tony," he said consolingly, " we've all got to live and learn. It wasn't too bad for a beginning, but, when coming to moorings, it's far better to get into neutral in good time and let her run her way out before you reach the buoy. If you do it too soon, you can easily shove the clutch in again and give her a bit of a kick ahead. It's ever so much better than coming up with a lot of way on and trusting to the reverse to stop her."

" Yes, I can see that now," admitted Tony. " But why did she turn away from the buoy? I had the tiller straight."

" Yes," chimed in Jack, who was as puzzled at the *Spray's* behaviour as his friend. " We were almost on top of the buoy and then she suddenly twisted right away from it."

"That's another thing," explained Tom. "You noticed that, when the engine was running ahead, she tended to turn to starboard and you had to give her a little bit of helm to counteract it. That is caused by the lower half of the propeller working in more solid water than the top half. Just the same thing happens when you go astern, only then, the propeller being in front, it has more effect. You notice it more when a boat is stopped than when she is travelling at a fair speed. It's just one of the little tricks that you have to know and allow for. You'll soon know them all when you've handled her for a few days. Now try again."

At their second attempt the boys were more successful. Jack declutched in good time, and Tony steered the *Spray* along so that she nosed right up to the buoy and he was able to leave the tiller, run forward and, leaning over the bow, grasp the buoy and hold it triumphantly aloft.

"Good work," said Tom Pascoe approvingly. "That was perfect. If you do it like that every time, you'll do well. Hullo, here comes the breeze."

The wind was indeed coming. Away to the south-east the calm surface of the sea was ruffled into dark patches which rapidly spread, and presently the solid line made by the advancing wind was visible behind them.

"Switch off!" cried Tony. "Let's sail."

Jack complied. The *Spray* was already stopped and lay inert on the water.

" I say," cried Jack, " isn't it quiet! I didn't realize what a row the engine was making."

" You can't make an engine in a boat afloat as quiet as you can in a car ashore," said Tom. " A boat is like a sounding-box. It magnifies all the sounds."

" I like sailing best," said Tony. " It beats motoring easily."

" I'll say what I think of sailing when I've done some," said Jack. " Motoring is very jolly, anyway. We shouldn't have got right out here without the motor."

" That's true enough," said Tom, as he unrolled the jib.

The breeze reached them at last and, with sundry creaks and groans from her gear, the *Spray* once more awoke into life; her sails filled and, lying over a little under the pressure of the breeze, she commenced to move through the water.

When it did arrive, the wind had " good heart ", as Tom called it, in it, and for another hour, with him again acting as the good-natured passenger, the boys sailed the *Spray* about the bay, tacking and manœuvring as he suggested. Intent on their work, the time passed quickly, and when Tom announced that it was time to return to moorings, both raised their voices in protest.

" Nay, nay," said Tom, smiling. " You can come out again this afternoon and to-morrow and the day after and every day for the rest of the holidays, when the weather's fit, and I expect you will, but I want my dinner, if you don't."

Still in the rôle of passenger, he watched them stow the jib and pick up the moorings, and as they rowed ashore they all agreed that the *Spray* was a lovely little ship and had acquitted herself splendidly on her trial trip.

CHAPTER IV

The Fog

It was nearly a week later. Tony and Jack had had a wonderful time since the *Spray* had sailed her trial trip. They had been afloat in her every day except one, which had been showery with a strong wind, when consideration for the new sails had kept them ashore. The *Spray* had fulfilled her early promise and had proved a great success, fast and handy under sail and a good sea boat. As old Bill Pascoe, her designer and builder, put it—" She's the sort of little craft that'll bring you home."

The engine, also, had given no trouble. Tom Pascoe had accompanied the boys for the first few days, becoming more and more of a genuine passenger, until at length he had told Major Bamford that, in reasonable weather, they were safe alone, and that it was simply wasting the Major's money and his own time to go with them any more; so, much to their delight, Tony and Jack were given permission to take the *Spray* out unaccompanied.

To their astonishment they found that they were not nearly so sure of themselves alone as they had been when there was a very competent " passenger " sitting

44

smoking his pipe, within call and ready to help in case of emergency. However, after a couple of sails in the bay they had quickly got over their nervousness and recovered their self-confidence, and now, with a well-filled luncheon basket and some fishing gear, they had sailed out to " the whiting ground ", where, rolling up the jib, they had let go the anchor for the first time.

It had seemed to require an awful lot of rope to get the anchor to the bottom, for the water was deep, but at long last the *Spray* had dropped astern and, when she was fairly riding to her cable, they had lowered the mainsail and commenced to fish.

Two other boats also lay at anchor a little distance away, both manned by professional fishermen, and in one of them Tony recognized his friend, young Sam Tonkin. They had exchanged friendly waves, but were too far apart to be able to communicate otherwise.

It was a glorious day and the time had passed quickly. At first the fish had refused to bite, but, with the turn of the tide, their luck had turned too, and for nearly an hour the fun had been fast and furious. With two lines apiece to attend to, the boys had been kept hard at work and the wooden fish-box which stood in the fore part of the well was almost full.

When the next lull came, they had eaten their lunch and had just stowed the remnants away in the basket.

" Hullo!" said Jack, standing up, after putting the basket back into the little cuddy. " Is that fog coming? I can't see the headland."

Tony looked up.

" You're right," he said. " That's fog, worse luck!"

At once he got out the little spirit compass with which the *Spray* was furnished, and, laying it on the seat, took a rough bearing of the cliff above the Wreckers' reef, three miles away.

" Nor'nor'west," he muttered, half to himself, as he checked his observation.

" What's that for?" demanded Jack, who had watched the operation with interest.

" That's the course we must steer to get home," explained Tony. " If it comes on really thick, we shan't be able to see the land or anything, and only the compass will keep us right. Being at sea is like being in the middle of a big field. There are no paths or signposts, but, if you know the direction of the gate, and can aim straight at it, you can get out all right. Our gate is the entrance to the cove and, now we know the course to steer, the compass will guide us to it."

" I see," said Jack, staring at the little card inside its neat mahogany box. " It's jolly interesting."

" I hope we shan't need the compass though," said Tony, a little uneasily. " The sea is worse than the field, after all, for the field does keep still, while the sea has tides and currents that may carry you right off your course, unless you know enough to allow for them. Perhaps the fog won't be very thick. It may just be a bank that will soon blow past."

" It looks to be a pretty big bank to me," said Jack.

He was right. The fog swept on like a white wall, blotting out the land as it came, and soon even the fishing boats had disappeared from sight and the *Spray* was enveloped in it. Save for a narrow circle of fifty yards or so of grey sea, the boys could see nothing.

" I say," said Jack, looking round, " this begins to feel rather funny."

His expression made Tony laugh.

" Yes," he agreed, " it does, rather, but it's quite all right, really. I've been out in fogs before with old Sam Tonkin. It's quite all right as long as you don't get lost. You must keep your reckoning of where you are."

" What happens if you do get lost?" asked Jack, " because, so far as I can see, we are lost now."

" Oh no, we're not," said Tony. " We know where we are, because we haven't moved, but if you move and then get lost, you have to anchor again—unless you like to take the risk of running on the rocks."

" Well, if we know where we are now," said Jack, " I vote we stay put."

" We can stay another couple of hours, anyway," said Tony. " There's no need to start back before five. It's low water about half-past, so the tide will be slack and there won't be any current to carry us out of our course. I say, pass my coat. This fog is jolly cold."

" I was just thinking the same," said Jack, passing

Tony's coat and donning his own as well. "Hullo!" he added, " I've got a bite."

Hauling in his line, he pulled a weird-looking fish to the surface, rather like a miniature shark. " Whatever's this?" he cried in astonishment.

" A dogfish," said Tony laconically.

" A dogfish," echoed Jack, as he swung his catch over the rail on to the floor of the well, where it squirmed and wriggled vigorously. " I've never seen one before. Is it good to eat?"

" No, not really. The fishermen used to throw them away, but I believe they sell them now, though they don't call them dogfish in the shops. They call them something else, so that the people won't know they're eating dogfish. If there are any more like him about, we may as well give up fishing. When they come along the other fish clear out."

" Why, do they eat them?" asked Jack.

" You bet they do," said Tony.

His prediction proved a correct one. Although they kept their lines out and hauled them up at intervals to make sure that the baits were all right, an hour passed without another bite.

" We shall have to think of moving soon," said Tony. " I wish this fog would clear a bit. It's a real thick one."

" So do I," agreed Jack. " We seem to be cut off from everywhere. We might be in the middle of the Atlantic. Hullo! what's that? Is it a motor-boat?"

Listening, the boys heard the sound of a distant

engine somewhere in the fog. The noise grew louder. Whoever it was, was coming nearer.

" Perhaps it is one of the fishermen, who has decided to go home," suggested Jack.

Tony shook his head.

" That's a more powerful engine," he said. " It's not a bit like the sound one of the fishermen's motors would make."

" You're right," agreed Jack; " it sounds more like a speedboat. I wonder who it is."

" Oh, it may be anyone," said Tony. " It's probably some yachtsman out for a run."

The noise of the engine grew louder. It was evident that the craft, whatever she was, was not very far away, and they strained their eyes vainly into the shrouding fog to try to make her out. Suddenly the noise ceased. The boys waited, still staring into the blankness of the fog, when they were startled to hear a double whistle, faint but quite distinct, sound out of the shrouding mists. It was answered by another, evidently a little closer, but still some distance away.

Tony and Jack looked at one another.

" That's very like the whistle we heard on the cliffs the other day," said Jack.

" I know," said Tony. In the excitement of his birth-day present, his suspicions had been forgotten, but now they returned with a rush. " It sounds to me like a signal. Hush! There it goes again!"

The whistle was repeated at intervals and the engine

could be heard running slowly. It seemed obvious that the whistle was being used as a guide.

" I wonder what the game is," said Jack. " Can it be one of the fishermen whistling to him?"

" It must be," said Tony. " There's no one else near."

Soon the whistles ceased and the boys heard a faint shout. The sound of the engine died away and for some minutes there was silence. Suddenly the motor restarted. This time the throttle was opened out. It sounded loudly for a time, then began to fade. The boat was evidently making off at full speed, and gradually the sound of her engine faded in the fog.

" I wonder what she was," said Jack.

" It wasn't a fisherman, I'm sure of that," said Tony, definitely. " None of them have a high-speed engine like that one. Of course, it may be some yachtsman who had got lost, and he saw the fishermen and spoke to them and, when they told him exactly where he was, he was able to shape a course to wherever he wanted to go."

" That explanation is all right as far as it goes, but what about the whistling?" queried Jack. " If the stranger went on until he saw the boats, he wouldn't need them to whistle to him as a guide. It seems a bit fishy to me."

" Yes," agreed Tony, " I think you're right there. I don't understand it."

" You'd better ask your friend Sam when we see him ashore. He may know all about it."

Tony started.

" Of course," he said, " it must have been Sam, or the other man. I didn't notice who the other was. He was farther away."

" Oh, well," said Jack, after a silence, " we don't know and all our talking won't find out for us. I know I wish this fog would go away. What time is it?"

" Five o'clock," said Tony, looking at his wrist watch. " We'd better be making a move. The tide is just right. It's as thick as ever, but it can't be helped."

Winding up their lines, they stowed them away in a locker and then set the mainsail. When all was ready, the two boys tailed on to the anchor warp. It was a hard pull. In the deep water of the fishing-ground, it was necessary to let out plenty of warp and there was a full twenty fathoms of it to haul in. It came fairly easily at first, after they had got the *Spray* moving, but gradually became more and more diffi-cult, until at last they were brought to a standstill.

" Whew! Let's have an easy," gasped Tony.

" What's the matter with it?" demanded Jack. " Is it stuck?"

" It's stuck all right. It must be foul of a rock or something," said Tony. " I'm afraid it's my fault. I ought to have remembered. Old Sam always scows his anchor when he brings up on this ground. It is a bit foul in places."

" What's ' scows the anchor ' ?" asked Jack.

" You make the warp fast to the crown, that's the wrong end really, and stop the bight of the warp to the ring, that's the proper end, with a bit of twine; then, when it gets stuck on a rock or something like this, and you heave short, as we have done, the twine breaks and the anchor comes away wrong end up quite easily."

" What shall we do now?"

" Have another try. Come on."

Lying well back, the boys put their weight on the warp, but failed to gain an inch.

" It's no good," said Jack at last. " We can't budge it. We shall have to cut it, or stay out here for ever," he added, laughing.

Tony was thoughtful.

" I don't want to lose the anchor the very first time we bring up," he said. " There's one thing we might try first. The motor might move it. Start her up, will you, Jack?"

While Jack got the motor running, Tony took a turn round the mast with the warp and belayed it under a pin.

" Now," he ordered, " put the clutch in and open her out."

Under the thrust of the screw the *Spray* surged ahead, then suddenly snubbed and her bow was depressed several inches by the strain of the warp, but the anchor still held stubbornly to its hold on the bed of the sea.

" Stop her," said Tony. " Now go astern."

Casting off the warp, he slacked away a few fathoms and made it fast again.

" Now go ahead."

Springing aft to the tiller, he pushed it hard over and the *Spray* described a half-circle.

" Stop her. Now, let's try again."

Once more the boys tailed on to the warp, to find that their manœuvre had been successful; the anchor was free and they were able to haul it up with ease.

" We may as well keep the engine running, now it's started," said Tony, when the warp had been made into a neat coil and hung up to drain and the anchor had been restowed under the floor-boards. " There's very little wind. It has dropped this last half-hour."

" How do you steer by compass?" asked Jack, as Tony, who took the tiller, kept glancing at the little card in its bowl on the seat before him.

" It's easy enough," said Tony. " That black line on the inside of the bowl is called the lubber's line and represents the ship's bow. We know our course to the cove is nor'nor'west, so we keep the nor'nor'west pointer on the card pointing to the lubber's line, which means that our ship is heading nor'nor'west, and that should take us clear of the Wreckers' reef and into the mouth of the cove."

For over half an hour, with her engine purring steadily, the *Spray* slipped over the calm sea, which was only slightly ruffled by the gentle north-easterly breeze. Tony at the tiller did his best to keep the nor'nor'west pointer glued to the lubber's line. They kept a good look-out all round, but, except for three or four cork floats marking some hidden crabpots at rest on the sea bed, they sighted nothing.

Presently Tony glanced at his wrist watch.

" We must be getting near. We might see something any time now, so keep your eyes skinned," he added professionally.

When another five minutes had passed and nothing had appeared to break the cold circle of grey sea which seemed to move along with them, he grew anxious.

" If the *Spray* does a good five knots, as Tom Pascoe said, we ought to be in the cove's mouth, for I know that the place where we anchored is not more than three miles out."

" There, what's that?" cried Jack, pointing to a dark object looming out of the fog on their starboard bow.

" It's a boat," said Tony. " She looks to be at anchor. We must be in the cove. Slow down. Hullo! what's that ahead?"

At that moment the *Spray* gave a sudden lurch that almost threw the boys off their feet and stopped dead.

" We're aground!" cried Tony. " Go astern. Full speed astern."

In his anxiety he leaped forward and threw the engine into reverse.

" Quick, help me get the sails down."

The jib was rolled up and the main and peak halyards let go, bringing the mainsail down with a run, then, casting off the mizzen sheet, Tony stood on the stern and, lifting the boom, effectually muzzled the little mizzen by wrapping it round the mast. Too late they realized that the other boat was not on her moorings, but aground also, though, drawing less water than the *Spray*, she was farther inshore in shallower water, her stern being some twenty feet ahead of the *Spray's* bow.

" Get the sweep out!" cried Tony, as he put a tyer round the bunt of the mainsail to keep it up out of their way. " We can push to help the engine."

The sweep was a big oar, lashed in place under the waterway, for use in case the motor refused duty in a calm. Using this as a quant, the boys tried to force the *Spray* astern into deeper water, but, strive as they might, they failed to move her.

" It's no good," panted Tony at last, lifting the sweep out of the water and laying it down on the deck. " She went on with such a rush that she's sued —that's lifted out of the water—quite a lot. We'll have to wait for the tide to float us off again. It won't be very long. It's lucky it isn't rough, or the sea would be bumping us about. I wonder where we are."

" Shall I stop the motor?" suggested Jack.

" You may as well. It isn't doing any good."

When the engine had stopped and the screw-driven water had ceased to sluice along her sides, the *Spray* lay peacefully with a slight list to port, and the boys had time to take full stock of their position. Luckily, as Tony had said, it was calm weather, so there was no danger. Also it was low water, so it would not be long before they were refloated by the rising tide.

" Why," said Tony, looking at the stranded fishing

boat, " that's the *Petrel*, Sam Tonkin's boat. I wonder where Sam is. There is no one aboard."

" I saw two men ahead of her just as we struck," he went on. " They were standing on the edge of the beach there. I'd just made them out, then in the excitement I never thought of them again until now. They've both disappeared. I wonder where they've gone."

" That's queer," commented Jack. " Surely they must have seen us."

" Hullo, Tony!" hailed a voice at that moment, and they saw the figure of a man emerging out of the mist.

He was clad in a fisherman's guernsey and long sea-boots and was wading along on the edge of the water.

" Is that you, Sam?" cried Tony. " How are you?" It was the first time he had met his friend these holidays.

" I'm all right, thanks," replied the young fisher-man, for it was he. " You look all right, too. That's a fine little vessel your father has had built for you. I like her."

" Yes, isn't she jolly?" cried Tony. " But what are you doing here, Sam, and where are we?"

Sam laughed.

" That's a question I might ask you, isn't it?" he responded banteringly. " We're ashore in Wreckers' Bay. How did you come to get here?"

" Wreckers' Bay!" repeated Tony, whose round eyes betrayed his surprise. " Then we're on the wrong side of the reef. We were making for the cove. I've made an awfully bad shot."

" Did you take a bearing before the fog came on?" asked Sam.

" Yes. Nor'nor'west, and I steered carefully too."

" What allowance did you make for the tide?"

" None. Low water is at half-past five, so it was just slack water, there was no need."

" Low water is at half-past six to-day," said Sam.

" No!" cried Tony, " I'm sure it isn't. I looked it out in the *Nautical Almanac* before we started. I know it's five-thirty."

" Ah," said Sam, " I think I see. Did you allow the extra hour for summer time? The almanac gives Greenwich time, for they don't recognize summer time at sea. You should have added an hour. Low water to-day is five-thirty by Greenwich time, but six-thirty by summer time, which is what your watch is set by."

" That's it, then!" cried Tony. " I couldn't understand how I got here. I thought it was slack water and all the time the ebb was carrying us westwards."

Sam nodded.

" It's lucky it carried you far enough to clear the reef. If you'd struck the rocks, going as hard as you struck these sands, you might have knocked a hole in your ship. That's another thing. Always ease down when you think you're getting handy to your port in a fog. However, as it happens, there's no harm done. The tide is coming now and we'll be afloat again directly."

During the conversation he had waded to his boat

and climbed in over the side. A few minutes later, with engines churning astern, the two boats backed off into deep water.

" I'm going in to moorings," shouted Sam, " so if you follow me, I'll lead you home."

Tony was glad enough to accept the offer, and so the *Spray* tailed on behind the *Petrel*. The two boats skirted the dreaded Wreckers' reef, passed close to the bell buoy which marked its extremity, and presently entered the little cove of Barlash. Shouting their thanks to their pilot, the boys headed the *Spray* for her moorings. They soon had her " moored up ", with the sails stowed away for the night, and rowed ashore in the dinghy.

. . . .

" Had a good day?" boomed Major Bamford from his study, as the boys, each with a string of fish dangling beside him, entered the hall. " I was beginning to wonder what had become of you, and if I should have to send out a search party—a relief ship, perhaps I ought to say—after you. This fog is pretty thick. How did you manage to find your way home?"

He listened with interest while the boys retailed their experiences.

" You were lucky to get off so lightly," he commented, as they wound up. " But what was young Sam Tonkin doing with his boat ashore there too? Surely he knows the place too well to get there by accident as you did."

" I don't know," said Tony.

" You asked him and he didn't say," said Jack. " He said he could just as well ask you the same question."

" So he did!" cried Tony. " I wonder what he was doing and I wonder who the other man was that he was talking to. What do you think, Dad?"

At that moment the gong boomed out its cheerful sound.

" Run along quickly and wash," said the Major. " Don't bother to change, or you'll be late for dinner."

When the boys had left him, he sat silent for a few moments, staring thoughtfully into the empty grate.

CHAPTER V

The Wreck

" There'll be no sailing for you to-day, boys," said the Major, as he settled himself at the breakfast table the next morning.

" No, I suppose it is too rough," agreed Tony regretfully.

Jack, muzzled by a mouthful of grapefruit, said nothing, but, from the expression of his face, it was obvious that he shared Tony's sentiments.

The fog had given place to a strong south-easter of almost gale force. Through the windows of the breakfast room the boys could see the trees bending and swaying in the wind and the clouds chasing each other in a mad race overhead.

" Whatever will you find to do with yourselves?" went on the Major chaffingly. " You'll have to give the *Spray* a rest. I should think she'll be glad of it, for you've certainly worked her pretty hard this past week."

The boys looked at each other.

" Well," said Tony hesitatingly, " we thought we might just go aboard her to put things straight. You

60

see, we were so late in getting to moorings last evening that we came ashore in rather a hurry."

" Yes," agreed Jack, " we didn't even wait to wash her down. She will be in rather a mess after the fishing."

Major Bamford laughed outright.

" Good," he said. " I'm glad to see that you intend to keep your ship clean and tidy, though I can't say that I've noticed any particular inclination on your part to do the same to your bedroom. I looked in last night, after you were asleep, on my way to bed, and your clothes were just two heaps on the floor."

The boys grinned a little sheepishly.

" Well," went on Major Bamford, " you ought not to come to any harm on the moorings, though you may find it a bit rolly, Jack. With the wind in this quarter, there is sure to be a biggish sea outside, and the swell will find its way into the cove. You'll probably find more motion to-day on the moorings than you felt out on the fishing grounds. Ever been seasick?"

" I'll chance that, sir," said Jack, laughing.

Old Bill Pascoe was surprised to see them launch their dinghy and prepare to row off to the *Spray*.

" You're never going to try it to-day, Master Tony," he protested. " Why, it's blowing nigh on a gale of wind and will be worse before it's better, or my name is not Bill Pascoe."

" No, Bill," laughed Tony, " not to-day. We're just going off to wash down and tidy her up a bit. We came ashore in a hurry last night."

" Oh, that's all right, then," said the kindly boat-builder in a relieved voice.

Aboard the *Spray* they found that the Major's prediction was a true one. There was plenty of motion, for though the cove was protected by the projecting point of rock and the stone breakwater so that there were no actual waves, yet the water was sufficiently disturbed to keep the little vessel in constant uneasy movement, sidling this way and that, and every now and again giving a smart tug at her mooring chain.

Tony was quite a seasoned salt, and, to his delight, Jack found that the swell did not affect him in the slightest.

Fishing is dirty work, and, however careful one may be, fish scales, bits of seaweed and slime are liable to get into nooks and crannies, where, if left undisturbed, they will soon begin to smell, so the boys set to work with a will.

Taking up the bottom boards, they gave the *Spray* a thorough cleaning. Tony scrubbed vigorously with the " tickler " while Jack baled up bucketfuls of clean salt water from overside and " sloshed " it about. When every likely cranny had been scoured out and everything washed down into the bilge, they baled and pumped out the water and mopped her dry, then they readjusted the boards and " chammied " all the varnishwork, drying it thoroughly.

They then turned their attention to the motor. First wiping away the oil and grease with a rag soaked in paraffin, they polished up the brasswork until it shone again, after which they wiped it lightly over with an oily rag and replaced the cover.

Having seen that all the sails and gear were properly secured to withstand the force of the growing wind, they rowed ashore and were surprised to find the boat-builder and his sons laying down their tools and putting on their coats. Busily employed, the time had passed quickly and they had no idea that it was half-past twelve and time " to knock off for dinner ".

As they walked back to the Hall, a drizzling rain began to fall.

" Old Pascoe was right when he said it would be worse before it was better," said Jack.

During luncheon they recounted to Major Bamford their doings of the morning.

" I ran across Mr. Temple in the village this morning," he said. " It seems there is a concert in the village hall this evening in aid of the new organ. I bought a couple of tickets. Here they are. You two had better go. It will be something to do to help you through a wet day."

" Why don't you come too, Dad?" asked Tony, a mischievous twinkle in his eye.

" I've got something more important to see to, young man," replied his father, with mock severity.

" What sort of a concert will it be?" asked Jack, when, lunch over, the boys were alone in the library.

" Very funny," said Tony, who had attended such entertainments before, " and it is not always the performers who mean to be funny who are the funniest.

It's jolly hard sometimes not to laugh out loud in the wrong place."

" I see," said Jack, his eyes gleaming in anticipation.

They spent the afternoon sprawled in big easy chairs, each with an exciting book on his lap, while the rain beat a tattoo on the window panes and the wind, growing gradually to a full gale, roared in the chimney.

The concert was timed to start at eight o'clock, and five minutes to the hour saw the two friends in their seats. The first part of the programme consisted of a series of songs and recitations and, as Tony had promised, most of them were amusing in one way or another and, though one or two of the items were a little " heavy going ", on the whole the boys thoroughly enjoyed themselves.

The second half of the programme was to be a farce, but the curtain had only just risen on the first scene when a loud explosion, like the report of a cannon, was heard in the night outside. The effect was electrical. Several men in the body of the hall rose to their feet, the actors on the stage ceased speaking and the whole audience waited in silence as though spellbound.

" What is it?" whispered Jack to Tony.

As though in answer to his question, a second report sounded. Instantly a babel of voices broke out and the audience rose in confusion.

" It's the signal for the lifeboat," said Tony. "There must be a vessel ashore, or in distress somewhere.

Quick. Get your mack on. We'll go and see the launch."

Slipping into their coats, the boys joined the throng which jostled its way to the exits. It was obvious that his sentiments were shared by the majority of the villagers. The play was forgotten, indeed two of the players were members of the lifeboat crew and had disappeared from the stage.

Once out in the street, all turned with one accord towards the lifeboat house and hurried along in an unruly procession. It was almost dark. Here and there a cottage door stood ajar with a woman standing silhouetted against the light of the lamp beyond, and maybe a small child clinging to her skirts or caught up in her arms, who stared with wondering eyes at the passing crowd.

Without exception, the men had answered the sudden call to duty with commendable promptitude, and their heavy seabooted feet clattered on the cobble-stones as they hurried along.

When the boys reached the lifeboat house, standing at the head of its long slipway, the big doors had already been thrown wide open and some of the crew were struggling into their oilskins and strapping on their cumbersome lifejackets. One by one they clambered up the ladder and took their places in the beautifully kept red, white and blue painted boat.

The ground helpers were doing their part.

" All ready?" cried the coxswain. " Stand by. Let her go."

The holdfasts were cast off, the rollers under the keel revolved as the boat began to move, and then, to a ragged but hearty cheer from the onlookers, the lifeboat roared down the slipway and took the water in a huge burst of spray. Almost as she touched the water, the oars straggled out and were soon dipping rhythmically, urging the boat out into the night on her errand of mercy.

" It was just like a waterchute on a big scale," commented Jack, who had watched his first lifeboat launch with intense interest.

Almost as he spoke there was a hiss and a wild splutter of sparks behind him, and, with a deafening roar, a rocket soared up into the night to carry a cheering message to the wrecked crew—that their signals of distress had been seen, that the lifeboat had been successfully launched and was even now on on its way to their assistance.

" Where is the wreck?" asked Tony of a bystander.

" On the Wreckers' reef," replied the man. " A steamer they say she be."

" On the Wreckers'," echoed Tony; " then we may be able to see her from the cliffs. Come on, Jack."

The boys started along the road as fast as they could push their way through the crowd, but presently were brought to a standstill, for the narrow street was completely blocked. Gradually working their way through to the front, they found that the obstruction was a peculiarly shaped lorry which, with a pair of horses in the shafts, was pulling out of a small building at the roadside.

" It's the rocket apparatus," said Tony; " with the breeches buoy, you know."

" Shall we follow it?" suggested Jack, when, having negotiated the turn, the vehicle set off at a smart trot down the street.

" No," said Tony, after a moment's thought, " they'll have to go round by the road. We can cut up the hill by the path. We'll be there before them easily."

They were not the only ones who took the steep path to the cliff, indeed some of the crew of the rocket brigade took the short cut also, but, with youth on their side, they were amongst the first arrivals at their goal.

Under the lee of the hill they had not felt the force of the wind, but as they reached the summit they met the full fury of the storm. For a moment it stopped them, staggering, in their tracks, but after the first shock they braced themselves and, leaning their weight against the wind, they fought their way to the cliff edge, where, half kneeling, half crouching on the turf in the scanty shelter afforded by a small gorse bush, they could see out over the black void and hear the storm-racked sea pounding at the cliff foot two hundred feet below. Guarding their eyes from the driving rain, they made out the lights of the distressed steamer, flickering points in the darkness.

" She's not on the Wreckers'," said a man's voice

beside them and, turning, they found that, unheard in the wild hurly-burly, a fisherman had approached and was sharing their meagre shelter. "She must have missed the rocks. She's right on the beach, I reckon."

The group grew in numbers as others arrived, panting and out of breath with their climb.

The gale battered them in heavy gusts, and the boys found that the rain, which beat a wild tattoo on their oilskins, was, under the relentless pressure of the wind, penetrating the " chinks of their armour "; a cold trickle found its way down their necks, while their shoes were soon completely soaked. Breathing was difficult, and they occasionally turned their backs to the gale to gain a temporary relief.

Presently the lights of the rocket brigade came into sight. With the horses straining in the shafts and the men heaving at the spokes of the wheels, the carriage was forced as far as possible up the steep hillside, but the last two hundred yards were impassable, and the gear had to be taken from the lorry and carried by hand.

With the aid of the many volunteers at hand, this was soon accomplished. Each man of the crew knew his job, and almost more quickly than it takes to tell the preparations were made, the rocket tripod was set up, the box of line and the heavy warps were laid out in position, while the spectators stood round in a wide semicircle to give them room.

A huge rocket was laid across the tripod with a

strong but light line attached to its stick. This line was arranged in a specially fitted box in such a way that it ran out freely without fouling.

When all was ready, the chief officer aimed the rocket at the wreck, making allowance for the slight angle of the wind, in much the same way as one would aim a cannon, and applied the sputtering squib. There was a pause, then in a burst of sparks the rocket roared its way out into the night against the gale.

Hundreds of eyes anxiously followed its course, and a simultaneous groan of disappointment sounded, even above the roar of the gale, when it was seen that, carried out of its course by the wind, the rocket had missed its mark.

No time was wasted. While some of the men hauled in the spent line, stowing it carefully, in and out, amongst the long wooden pegs in its box in case it were required again, a second rocket was set up with a spare line attached to it.

With the knowledge gained by his first failure, the chief officer " laid " the rocket on its stand. Again the squib sputtered, again the tense moment of waiting, and again came the sudden burst of sparks, in the midst of which the rocket took flight, roaring its way out against the gale. This time the aim was perfect. Straight and true it flew for its mark, right over the wreck, to finally plunge into the sea a hundred feet beyond.

" Good shot!" cried half a dozen voices and, with a long-drawn " a-ah ", the watchers breathed their relief.

A wait followed, then the thin line, which led over
the edge of the cliff into the black void, began to move.
The crew of the distressed steamer had found it and
were hauling it in.

A pulley-block, with a " whip ", or endless rope,
rove through it, was already attached and, with the
men carefully easing it away, was hauled out to the
wreck.

The block had a slip of wood attached to it on which
were painted instructions in several languages, and
presently a flashing light on the vessel signalled that
the instructions—to make fast the block high up on
the mast, or some other strong and solid part of the
wreck—had been carried out.

" Haul away," ordered the chief officer.

" Here," said a burly helper, " give us a hand, will
ye?"

Glad to be of real use, the boys tailed on to the rope
and pulled with a will. A heavy hawser was made fast
to the other part of the whip and was hauled out to
the wreck. This also had a board of instructions tied
on it and, after awhile, the light again signalled that all
was well and that the hawser had been made fast—a
few feet above the block.

While this had been going on, other helpers had
buried an anchor deep in the turf, and now the hawser,
being kept off the ground by a heavy steel tripod, was
hauled taut by willing volunteers and finally, by means
of blocks and tackle, " set up " tightly to the anchor,
so that it stretched in a sagging curve, but well above

the raging breakers, from the cliff-top to the wreck.

The rest was easy. The breeches buoy, a lifebelt with a huge pair of " shorts ", made of stout canvas, sewn to it, was slung on the hawser by a pulley and, by means of the whip, hauled out to the wreck.

A flare now flamed up in the night beyond the steamer. It was the lifeboat. She had fought her way out of the bay, round the headland and to windward of the wreck against the full fury of the storm, and was preparing to let go an anchor and drop down on the steamer. It would have been a manœuvre fraught with great danger and, as the rocket brigade had established communication, a needless one, so the chief officer burned a flare in reply, signalling that he could save the crew and that the lifeboat's services were not required.

Again the flashing light on the steamer pierced the darkness. Tony and Jack stood waiting, letting the rope slip freely through their fingers, while helpers, pulling on the other side of the whip, hauled the breeches buoy ashore again, but now it was no longer empty, for the youngest member of the shipwrecked crew, his legs dangling through the shorts, was seated in it.

Eager hands reached out to him as he was hauled over the cliff edge. He was helped out and, bobbing and swaying, back into the darkness went the now empty buoy.

So the work of rescue went on. The boys did their share, alternately hauling on the rope which carried the empty buoy out to the wreck, and letting it slip through their hands as another member of the crew was hauled shore. Once a sympathetic laugh went up when, in the glare of the lanterns which lit up the scene, it was seen that one of the crew had the ship's cat snuggled safely in his arms. It, too, was lifted into safety.

When the buoy had made no less than eighteen double journeys between the ship and the shore, the captain himself, last to leave his charge, was hauled to safety over the cliff edge, the ship's papers buttoned inside his coat.

It was all over. There was nothing more to be done, so, while the shipwrecked crew, in charge of the local representative of the Shipwrecked Mariners' Society, were cared for in the village, Jack and Tony, soaked to the skin but supremely happy, made the best of their way back to the Hall, where Major Bamford, seeing their condition, ordered hot baths and hot lemon drinks, during the sipping of which he sat on Tony's bed and listened to their account of the evening's adventure.

CHAPTER VI

The Salving of the Steamer

The boys slept soundly and awoke the next morning none the worse for their soaking. The gale had continued with unabated violence throughout the night, but about six o'clock in the morning, during an extra heavy squall, the direction of the wind had changed, so that now, having veered to the north-west, it was blowing off the land, instead of on to it.

As soon as breakfast was over the boys hurried back to the cliff. The steamer was still there, but even nearer to the foot of the cliff, having driven farther inshore as the tide rose. To their surprise, save for a smashed boat hanging drunkenly in the davits, she showed no sign of damage.

The sea, no longer driven in by the wind, had subsided to a heavy swell, which, mounting higher and higher as it neared the shallow water, finally curled over and broke with a thunderous roar that rose and fell in volume but was never entirely hushed.

A little knot of men were standing on the cliff about the lifeline, which was still in position, while others could be seen on the steamer itself. In the offing lay three stump-masted, high-funnelled, bluff-bowed tugs, rolling in the trough of the swell.

"Morning, young gentlemen. Have you come to see the fun?"

The boys turned to find Tom Wallis beside them.

"There's the carcass," he went on, "and there are the vultures come for the pickings."

"What is it?" asked Tony. "What are they here for?"

"For what they can get," grinned Tom. "Two came along before daylight, gale or no gale. I could see their lights from the Watch House, and the other has just arrived. It's salvage they're after. If they can pull the vessel off, they'll make a tidy little sum."

"Will they be able to do it?"

"Can't say," responded the coast-guard, with a shrug of the shoulders. "They say she isn't badly holed and has made scarcely any water. It depends on how far she was drove up with the tide this morning. The wind was onshore then."

"Who are the men aboard her?" asked Jack.

"The crew have gone back aboard and some fellows from the shore as well to lend them a hand."

"How did she come to get ashore?" asked Jack.

"The gale. She was bound around the land to load coal at Cardiff, or one of those South Wales ports, and the gale caught her. Flying light in ballast, like she was, she'd be almost unmanageable when it got really bad. The skipper let go his anchors, but they didn't hold, or else he left it too late. See the chains from her bow?"

" She must have made some water. I see they're pumping her out," said Tony, referring to the steady stream of water that was pouring from a pipe hole in her side.

" They say hardly any," said Tom. " Being light, she wouldn't bump so heavy, and the sand is not all that hard. That water you see coming out of her is from her water ballast tanks, I reckon. They're pumping it out to lighten her all they can, so she'll float easier. Well, so long. I've just done my spell and am off home for a bit of shut-eye. She won't float before high water. That's about three o'clock."

Fearful of missing the actual refloating, the boys rushed home for some sandwiches and then settled down to spend the morning on the cliff, watching the preparations for the salvaging of the steamer. Save when heavy squalls occasionally drove up out of the north-west, when the sky became overcast and the rain pelted down in torrents, the day was fine enough.

As the tide rose, the tugs came nearer and, with the help of two of the local fishing boats, stout hawsers were carried from the vessel to each tug.

The experts who had surveyed the vessel's position had decided that she would come off stern first, if she came off at all, so two of the tugs had their tow ropes made fast to the stern, while the third had hers to the bow, to keep it from driving farther inshore.

The crew of the steamer had relit the fires, which

they had drawn before leaving her the previous night, and as time passed a wisp of steam could be seen issuing from the steam pipe, telling of plenty of pressure ready for use. Water no longer poured from the hole in her side, and it was evident that, her ballast tanks having been pumped dry, there was little water in her.

As the time of high water drew near, the steamer began to stir in her bed of sand, rolling uneasily as the swells swept past her and drew groans of protest from the tortured hull. The tugs worked into position, their propellers turning slowly ahead to keep them in their proper station. Excitement amongst the on-lookers grew as the time passed, with the tide gradually rising higher and higher, and the question, Would it rise high enough to float her? was discussed and re-discussed.

The gale of the previous night had caused an extra high tide, and the wiseacres amongst the fishermen, who had gathered on the cliff to watch, as the crucial time drew near, differed in their opinions as to how much the tide would " cut " now that the wind had veered into a different quarter. The boys listened with all their ears.

At long last the " zero hour " arrived. It was now or never. The tugs began to steam their hardest while from the winch on the steamer's forecastle came a burst of steam. They were heaving in on the two anchors, whose cables led seaward from the bows, trying to help.

The minutes passed and still the steamer refused to

leave her bed of sand. It seemed like checkmate. Then there was a stir amongst the group of sightseers on the cliff-top when the huge bow was seen to move seaward a little as it lifted on a swell.

Man proposes, but the forces of nature are sometimes too much for him. The vessel was more willing to come off bow first than stern first, as the experts had expected. She swung her bow through twenty degrees and then hung, refusing to move farther.

One of the tugs let go her hawser to the stern and, manœuvring into a new position, got a towrope to the bow, where she added her power to that of her partner, which all the time kept up her steady strain.

" No good. She ain't going off this tide," commented an old fisherman, after a few minutes had passed without further movement on the part of the steamer. " Tide's on the turn now. It won't rise no higher."

The words were barely out of his mouth, when the huge bow moved again, swung farther seaward, and, the tugs pulling more in line with her bow, she slid ahead a few feet as a swell surged past. Again she slid ahead, stopped, slid ahead again, hesitated, and, in a final burst, slid off the beach into deep water as a ragged impromptu cheer rose from the watchers on the cliff, in which the shrill voices of our friends could be plainly heard.

The lifeline of the rocket apparatus, which had been kept connected, but slacked down, until the last in case of failure, was let go aboard the steamer and, as she towed away to the safety of deep water, the coast-guardsmen commenced to haul in the lines and restow them in their boxes. Tony and Jack gladly lent their friends a helping hand and, by the time they had finished their self-imposed task, the steamer, with her attendant tugs grouped like satellites around her, was already growing small in the distance.

" Where are they taking her?" asked Jack.

" Plummermouth, I expect," said one of the coast-guard. " There is a dry dock there. They'll want to look her over and put her to rights before she goes to sea again. She's lucky she didn't strike the Wreckers'. If she had ha' done—and she could only just have missed—she wouldn't ha' got away as easy as she done this morning. She'd ha' been there for keeps, I reckon."

CHAPTER VII

The Unexpected Storm

" I vote we have another sail in the *Spray*," said Tony a couple of days later.

The boys were breakfasting alone, for Major Bamford had gone up to London the previous morning and was not expected back until the afternoon.

" I'd love to, but isn't it blowing a bit hard?" said Jack, looking out of the window at the swaying trees.

" Yes, it is a bit fresh, but nothing to hurt," agreed Tony. " It's blowing off the land, so the water will be smooth enough, even if the wind is strong. If we reef, we shall be all right."

" Shall we fish again?" asked Jack.

" Better not," decided Tony. " The fishing ground is nearly three miles off shore. Plenty far enough for the sea to get up for a little ship like the *Spray*. We had better keep close to the land, then we'll have shelter. We won't go far."

After breakfast, armed with a luncheon basket, they set off for the village. The boatbuilder's yard was deserted as they passed through, for Bill Pascoe and his sons were at work aboard a little trading ketch anchored in the cove.

Getting into their dinghy, the boys rowed off to the *Spray*.

" We shan't need the motor to-day," said Jack, as the fresh breeze ruffled the surface of the landlocked cove into tiny wavelets.

" No fear," said Tony. " We'd better put a couple of reefs in the mainsail, I think."

Twenty minutes later they were under way. As they sailed out of the cove they passed the little coaster in which Bill Pascoe was at work. He came up on deck as they left her astern, and, after staring at them for a few moments, shouted something which they could not catch. Tony waved his arm in reply.

" What did he say?" asked Jack.

" I don't quite know. Something about mind something ' don't fly on us '. There are no flies on us," he added facetiously. " Perhaps he was warning us not to go out to the fishing grounds."

Outside the cove they hauled in the sheets and stood along the shore. Close to the land, as Tony had predicted, there was good shelter and the water was smooth, while the wind sent the *Spray* flying along at a glorious speed in spite of the reefs. They sailed about a mile and then, putting about, sailed back again.

" This is jolly!" cried Jack. " It's the best sail we have had."

" Isn't it?" agreed Tony. " I say, it's quite okay

in the shelter of the land; let's sail along the coast to Boldrington Bay. It's only about ten miles. It's a topping little place. We could anchor there and have our lunch. We might bathe, too."

" Good," agreed Jack, " let's."

The little yawl slipped along in fine style, heeling exhilaratingly to the stronger puffs and reeling the miles off behind her in quick time. It took them barely a couple of hours to reach the little bay.

It was a queer, horseshoe - shaped indentation in the cliff, rather like a bowl, with one side broken away. There were no " snags ", as Tony put it, in the entrance, and, though the wind was baffling under the high land, they soon managed to beat in and let go their anchor in the middle of the pool.

In spite of the recent bad weather, the water was so clear that they could see the fine sandy bottom a few feet below the keel. They stowed the sails and then, stripping off their clothes, were soon in the water. Both boys could swim well, but Tony was really expert and several times swam under the *Spray* to bob up on the other side.

After their swim they ate their lunch and then sprawled in the bottom of the boat, where, sheltered from the wind, they could sunbathe in comfort.

" I say!" Jack, who had been lying flat on his back, suddenly sat up. " Look at that cloud."

Tony had been idly inspecting the little coupling on the shaft of the engine, but he looked up at Jack's words, to see the ragged edge of a black cloud rising over the cliff-top. He scrambled to his feet and stood up, looking just a trifle uneasy.

" What is it?" asked Jack. " A squall?"

" Looks like it," said his chum, " and a pretty nasty one too."

" What had we better do? Stay put till it's over?"

Tony shook his head.

" Start for home under the engine, I think. This cove is so shallow that, if the wind changed and blew onshore, we should be in the breakers. It's only good with an offshore wind."

As they got the engine started, a few drops of heavy rain fell. They put on their oilskins before hauling up the anchor, and headed for the open sea.

What a change had come over the scene when they emerged from the bay and opened up the long line of coast! On their trip up, the cliffs had appeared warm and friendly, while the blue of the sky above was reflected in the deeper blue of the sea below, which, ruffled by the breeze, had shown here and there the snowfleck of a little " whitecap ". Now, with heavy clouds banking up over the land, the cliffs looked grim and gloomy, and the sea, no longer a cheerful blue, had assumed a drab grey.

Even as they watched, the distant coastline was swallowed up in a grey curtain of falling rain which swept along the land and out over the sea towards them. As it approached, the seething hiss of the rain-drops striking the water could be plainly heard. The wind grew stronger, coming in fierce puffs, and suddenly, as the rain reached them, they were enveloped in a deluge of falling water of almost tropical violence that blotted out land and sky and left them hemmed in on a narrow circle of windswept sea.

" I say," said Jack, who was at the tiller, looking out, as well as he could in the pelting rain, from under the brim of his sou'wester, " I can't see a thing. I hope I'm heading right."

For answer, Tony disappeared into the little cuddy, to reappear a moment later with the compass, which he placed on the seat by Jack's side.

" I'm not sure," he said, " but I think the course is about west by south. Steer that, anyway. It can't rain as hard as this for long, and then we'll be able to see the coast again. It isn't all that far away, although we can't see it."

For half an hour the little *Spray* chugged along on her course, throwing the spray, her namesake, over her bluff bows in clouds, though, except for the taste of salt in their mouths, the boys could scarcely distinguish it from the rain.

" The rain's easing," said Tony at last. " I'm sure it's not as heavy as it was."

" Is that a bit of cliff showing?" asked Jack. " I fancy I can make out——"

He never finished his sentence, for at that moment the motor suddenly stopped dead. The chums looked at one another.

" The rain has got at the ignition, I expect," said Jack.

Leaving the useless tiller, he stepped forward and, slipping the catch, made to lift the cover of the engine casing.

" Wait a minute," said Tony. " You'll only let more water in."

Lifting a portion of the mainsail, he laid it across the well to form a rough shelter for Jack and the engine.

" Now go ahead," he said, holding it in position.

Jack slipped off the cover and, unscrewing a plug connexion, held it close to the plug while he pulled the engine over.

" It seems all right," he said. " I'll try the other."

The second gave equally satisfactory results.

" The ignition seems okay," said Tony. " See if she'll start."

Jack tried her half a dozen times, finally swinging the handle vigorously. There was no result.

" Let me try," suggested Tony.

They changed places, but Tony's efforts were as unsuccessful as his chum's.

" What about the petrol?" suggested Jack.

With a startled exclamation, Tony tested the carburettor.

" I say, it's getting a lot rougher," said Jack, who stood up and looked round as he did so.

" There's no petrol," said Tony, ignoring his friend's remark. " Sound the tank."

" It's empty," said Jack, having twice dipped the little notched stick into the tank and withdrawn it, dry.

"That's done it," cried Tony. "I knew we must be getting short after our last day out. I took the can ashore to bring off some more, but I never worried about it this morning. With a jolly good breeze like this going, I didn't think we should need it."

"There's wind enough, all right," said Jack, "look how big the waves are."

"While we've been fooling with the engine, we've been drifting out to sea," said Tony. "Goodness knows how far we are off the land, but some distance judging by the size of the waves. Come on. There's no time to waste. Put the cover on the engine. We must set sail again."

But before the mainsail could be set, another reef had to be taken in, for the wind was very strong, then, to balance the three reefs in the mainsail, the small jib had to be set instead of the large one. All this took time, during which the *Spray*, driven by the storm, drifted farther and farther out to sea.

At last the sails were set and, taking the tiller, Tony steered the boat close hauled on the starboard tack, which, had the wind been in its old quarter, would have carried them in the direction of home on a course which gradually converged with the coast. In the bustle of setting sail, Tony had slipped the compass into the stern locker, to protect it from accidental damage, and, thinking he was heading in the right direction and requiring all his wits about him to nurse the little yawl safely through the heavy squalls, he never gave it another thought.

Alas, with the coming of the rain, the wind had gradually " backed ", changing its direction a few points, so that they were no longer heading for their port and gradually converging with the land, as Tony thought, but were actually edging farther and farther away from the land and out to sea.

CHAPTER VIII

Blown Out to Sea

The rain had certainly eased and was now nothing more than a steady downpour, but the wind kept up its relentless force. Even with the reduced sail the gallant little *Spray* was hard pressed, and Tony, with an arm crooked round the tiller and the end of the mainsheet, turned under the cleat, in his hand, had to use all his skill to keep his charge from being over-powered or filled by the heavy seas.

Jack sat to windward, amidships, using his weight to help the yawl to " stand up ", as Tony had so often heard old Sam call it, but soon he had another duty—that of working the pump, for, in addition to the rain and spray, an occasional " dollop " of solid water would tumble in over the weather gunwale and find its way into the bilge, where the quantity of accumulated water was beginning to make itself felt, and even to be seen above the floor-boards as the little ship lurched extra heavily to leeward.

" I can't make it out," said Tony at last, in a puzzled voice. " We ought to be getting nearer to the coast, but, though the rain is not nearly so bad and we can see quite a distance at times, there isn't a sign of land anywhere."

" The waves seem to be getting bigger," said Jack, as another comber tumbled aboard and crashed into the well.

" That's what's worrying me," said Tony. " If we were getting nearer to the shore, they would be getting less, instead of bigger. Are we making an awful lot of leeway, or what? It's blowing harder than it was, and we've precious little sail set, but she seems to be getting along through it all right in spite of it."

" Where's the compass?" he asked a minute later, as an idea occurred to him.

Jack found it eventually, after a search, for they had forgotten where they had put it and looked for it in its proper place, in the cuddy, and put it on the seat in front of the helmsman. Tony studied it, as the card gradually settled to a reasonable steadiness, and then gave a gasp of dismay.

" I say," he said, " the wind must have shifted quite a lot. We are not heading anything like west by south. We're barely sailing sou'west. If it's been like this for long, we must be miles out to sea."

" What shall we do, then?" asked Jack. " Tack ship?"

Before Tony could answer, the *Spray* sank in the deep hollow preceding an extra big wave. Tall and steep, with little " foot " to it to give the hard-pressed little vessel a chance to rise to meet it, it towered over them, its curling crest toppling and breaking in a white smother of foam.

Tony pushed the tiller down to try to help his charge to surmount the obstacle, but he was too late. The crucial moment had passed while his attention was distracted by the compass. The gallant little yawl did her best, lifting her bow boldly to her enemy, but it was more than she could accomplish. The wave surged over the weather gunwale, a solid mass of water, and poured into the cockpit like the breaking of a dam.

At first the boys thought that the end had come, for, until some of the water found its way below the floor-boards, it was almost up to their knees. Half-waterlogged, the little *Spray* lurched drunkenly down the back of the wave. Instinctively, Tony had let go the sheet, and, realizing that they were still afloat, he grappled splendidly with the situation.

" Roll up the jib," he shouted to Jack, and, while his friend obeyed, he sprang for the halyards and let the mainsail down with a run.

" Pump!" he shouted. " Pump for your life!"

Jack needed no second bidding. He realized their case was desperate. Seizing the pump handle, he pumped as he had never pumped before, sending a steady stream of water gushing overboard, while Tony put a rough but secure lashing round the lowered mainsail, and then, pulling up some of the floor-boards, he seized the bucket and commenced to bale with might and main.

For a few minutes it was touch and go. Carrying her heavy load of water, the *Spray* rose sluggishly to the waves, but, with no sail save the diminutive mizzen to press her down, she managed to lurch drunkenly over them. Some slopped aboard at first, and for a time the boys seemed unable to make any impression on the volume of water swirling about in the bilges, but gradually they gained the upper hand, and as the *Spray*, freed of the deadweight, gained freeboard and became more lively, so less water found its way aboard. At last Tony was able to lay aside his bucket and take stock of the situation.

" Shall we set the mainsail again?" asked Jack, still working away at the pump handle.

Tony looked to windward at the waves, grim and threatening, marching up, rank on rank, out of the greyness, and heard the whistle of the wind in the rigging, now risen to a shrill note.

" We might, but I don't think she'd work to windward through that sea," he said doubtfully.

" What then?" asked Jack. " Just let her drift? Where will we blow to?"

" Out to sea," said Tony ruefully. " But we can make her drift more slowly and perhaps keep her quieter too. Come on."

Jack only wanted the lead of his more experienced chum, and seconded his efforts manfully.

Pulling out the anchor and warp, Tony bent the anchor on without stocking it.

" Will the anchor hold out here?" asked Jack doubtfully.

" Too deep," said Tony. " The anchor will never reach the bottom, but we don't want it to. The pull of the warp through the water will check her drift a bit. Let go."

The anchor was tumbled over the weather bow with a double warp made fast to it. At first it appeared to have no effect, but gradually the *Spray* headed more towards the wind and, taking the seas broad on the bow, instead of wallowing broadside on in the troughs, rode more easily, though the spray still pelted the boys with monotonous regularity, while now and again a wave top tumbled over the rail and, though most of it ran harmlessly across the deck forward and out of the lee scuppers, some of it found its way into the well.

It was an uncomfortable and difficult situation, fraught with dire peril. A half-decked boat, far at sea in a gale of wind and drifting farther and farther away from port and safety. The farther from the sheltering land, the larger might grow the waves, which tumbled and crashed in every direction. Fascinated, the boys watched them rolling by. To the casual glance they appeared much alike, but when closely studied the difference in their formation was obvious.

Some had an easy slope with a rounded top, and these the *Spray* surmounted, passing over the crests, with deck free from water. Others had less base and, being steeper, were harder to climb. Some seemed to come from more ahead, while others struck broad on the beam. Here and there a wave could be seen rising higher and higher, its mounting crest growing thinner and thinner, until at last, unable to maintain its balance,

it toppled and broke in a smother of foam. These were
the dangerous waves, and the boys watched them
anxiously, if they threatened to break as they neared
the *Spray*. While some broke against the bow and
tumbled aboard a mass of solid water, for the most
part the *Spray* was lucky, though one monster wave
only toppled and broke just in time ahead of the little
vessel. Though its force was spent, for a moment the
little yawl seemed afloat in a sea of foam.

So the afternoon passed in ceaseless anxiety for the
boys and evening drew on.

" Perhaps the gale will die at sunset," said Tony,
voicing a hope that he did not think likely to be fulfilled,
as he took his spell at the pump, which they worked
turn and turn about.

" I hope so," said Jack. " Hullo! what's that?"

All the afternoon they had been alone on their
patch of grey sea, but now a tall shape was emerging
out of the mist.

" It's a steamer," cried Jack. " And heading
straight for us."

" They'll pick us up," said Tony joyfully, then his
face fell as he realized with sudden dismay that the
promised safety could only be obtained at the cost of
the loss of his beloved *Spray*. They would have to
abandon her.

But it was no use thinking of that. He steeled his
heart. The danger was urgent. One unlucky wave
breaking on top of them might fill the well to the brim
and send them to the bottom like a stone.

Yes, it was a steamer. As she drew nearer, she showed herself to be a big white steam yacht with a tall yellow funnel. She was driving easily ahead into the gale, her flaring bows thrusting scornfully aside the waves which threatened the little *Spray* with destruction.

Standing up on the thwarts and holding on with one hand, the boys waved their sou'westers vigorously. At first there was no response, and they thought they were not seen, then an arm flourished for a moment above the weather cloth on the bridge, and a short deep " toot " sounded from the whistle. The vessel's way eased, her engines had evidently been stopped, but the momentum of her deadweight carried her on so that she finally came to a standstill about sixty yards to leeward of the *Spray*.

As she fell off into the trough of the sea, two figures could be seen mounting the ladder to the bridge, to join the man already there in what seemed to be a consultation.

From their tossing craft, the boys watched eagerly. One of the men seemed to be urging something which the others refused to consider. Finally the two who had ascended to the bridge climbed down the ladder again and disappeared into a deckhouse. The other, who appeared to be the captain, stared in their direction for a time and then turned away. A few moments later, to the boys' consternation, the propeller began to churn the water under the stern and the yacht gathered way.

Hardly able to believe their eyes, the boys began to wave again, but their signals of distress were ignored; the man on the bridge stared steadfastly ahead over the weather cloth, and the steam yacht, steadily gathering speed, was soon lost to sight in the shrouding rain, leaving the boys with a feeling of forlornness as they gazed from their tiny craft at the wind-tormented sea.

CHAPTER IX

The End of the Gale

" What cads! What ghastly cads!" cried Tony indignantly when at last he realized that the steamer had indeed deserted them.

" Why did they do it?" demanded Jack, no whit less indignant. " Do they think we are all right?"

" I'm sure they don't," said Tony scornfully. " It's more likely they were afraid to launch a boat, but they need not have worried. We could have got the *Spray* alongside them. Dear old *Spray*," he added, after a pause. " I'm almost glad, in a way, that they have left us."

" Um," grunted Jack, in a noncommittal tone, as a wave-top surged aboard and tumbled, with a heavy splash, into the well, and he turned to work the pump.

Luckily for the boys, the weather was mild, and though they were wet to the skin they did not feel cold. Presently, however, they began to feel hungry, in spite of their anxiety, and, collecting the remnants of their lunch—some cake, two apples and a banana— they made a makeshift meal and felt all the better for it.

" Good!" cried Jack suddenly.

" What is?" demanded Tony, looking round to see

what had caused his chum to make his joyful exclamation.

" It's full moon to-night, so it won't be all that dark," Jack explained.

" A fat lot of use the moon will be, with all this rain. Hullo, though, I say, I believe it's stopping at last and, look, the sky is breaking. Perhaps it is going to ease up at sunset after all."

Half an hour later an angry ball of a sun sank out of the clouds through a narrow strip of clear sky on the horizon into the sea below. There was no doubt about it, the wind was definitely easing at last and veering again more northerly.

" I believe we could sail now," said Tony some time later, after carefully scanning the sea to windward.

" All right, let's try it," agreed the ever-ready Jack.

So the mainsail was hoisted, the jib unrolled and the anchor hauled in over the bows. Tony again took the tiller and trimmed the mainsheet.

The waves were still alarmingly big, but, without the weight of wind behind them, were no longer as dangerous as they looked. Over the watery hills and into the watery valleys the little *Spray* climbed and fell, climbed and fell with monotonous regularity. Tony put her on the port tack and stood in on a long leg. Gradually the daylight faded and it grew dark and presently, far away to windward, a light flashed and flashed again at regular intervals. Tony watched it for a while.

" That must be the Bellows lighthouse," he said.

"We must have drifted an awful long way out to sea. I should think the light is fifteen miles away and dead to windward too. It will take us all night to beat back against the wind."

"I don't care how long we are, as long as we do get back," said Jack cheerfully. "A couple of hours ago I was wondering if we should be feeding the fishes by this time. Whew, that was a big one!"

Magnified by the darkness, the waves appeared bigger than by daylight, and it was more than a little eerie for the boys, inexperienced as they were in night work at sea, to sail their little ship under such conditions.

But the gale was over. The wind was definitely lighter, nothing more, in fact, than a good breeze, and presently they dared to shake out two of the reefs. The *Spray* felt the extra canvas and became a thing of life, flitting from crest to crest like a swallow.

Darkness plays queer tricks on the senses and not only do waves appear larger, but, by night, boats appear to sail faster, and to Tony and Jack their little craft seemed simply to fly along.

"I say, she is going, isn't she?" said Jack, a trifle uneasily, for, as she crashed down into the hollows, with the next wave towering up ahead of her, it seemed as though she might easily plunge straight to the bottom.

But familiarity is said to breed contempt and, as time went on and their little vessel continued to surmount the seas unharmed, confidence returned in full force and they were even able to enjoy their unexpected experience. Though still hidden by the clouds, the light of the moon penetrated their veil to some extent, making the night less dark than it would otherwise have been.

They worked to windward in long tacks, putting about every half-hour or so. It was a long time before the lighthouse on Bellows Point seemed to get any nearer, but it served as a guide, a target at which to aim, for they knew that Barlash Cove was only some two miles along the coast to the eastward of it. Its beam was friendly and comforting, too, and they felt happier, knowing their comparative position, than they would have done had there been nothing but the dark water all around them. For the most part they had the sea to themselves, though twice they saw the lights of distant steamers and once some huge liner, her lights gleaming " like a grand hotel ", passed within a mile of them.

" I say, I'm getting sleepy," announced Jack with a yawn.

" Well, why not curl up in the cuddy?" suggested his chum.

" What, and leave you out here alone?" cried Jack indignantly. " That wouldn't be fair."

" I can manage," said Tony. " There's really nothing to do except steer, now there's no need to pump. You might just as well turn in."

" That's so," agreed Jack. " And if we could take it turn and turn about, I'd agree, but I'm not a good enough helmsman yet to be left alone in this sea. I know that, so I'm staying out here with you; thanks all the same."

Nothing would shake him in his resolve and, in spite of all Tony's arguments, he insisted on remaining " on deck " as he called it.

" It's a pity we haven't a tin of petrol," he said, after a time. " It would get us to windward quicker than sailing, seeing that sailing against the wind we have to zig-zag about such a lot. Why, we must cover twice the distance it is as the crow flies."

" That's true enough," laughed Tony. " But if we'd had a tin of petrol we shouldn't have been out here at all. We'd have been on the moorings long ago."

Slowly the night passed and, as time went on, it became obvious that they were gaining ground—the lighthouse was definitely nearer. The sea was calming down, too, and now they were sailing over nothing worse than a long, smooth swell.

Dawn came at last. First a faint lightening in the eastern horizon, which gradually spread to the zenith above, and presently the light came creeping shyly over the sea. In the east the clouds had broken up and the sky near the sea rim was clear, glowing in tints of pearly grey that gradually warmed to pink before Old Sol himself popped his head up over " the edge of the world " to send a path of shimmering gold along the surface of the water till it almost touched the *Spray*. Once in sight, the sun rose swiftly and soon sailed clear, while the tints faded, and, almost before the boys realized it, the night had gone and it was full day.

"Land ho!" cried Tony, pointing to windward.

Land it was. Shrouded in the white mists of morning, about three miles away, were the high cliffs of the coast to the east of Barlash.

"That will be the cove," said Tony. "In there, under that conical hill. We'll be ashore in time for breakfast, I do believe."

"I'm jolly glad to hear it!" cried Jack. "I shall be ready for it, I know. Just think—bacon and eggs and coffee—Ooh!"

"I'm pretty empty myself," admitted Tony. "Hullo, there's another boat out," he added a little later, pointing to a distant sail far away to the westward of them.

"So there is," said Jack. "What is she?"

"It'll be a fisherman, I expect," said Tony. "Out early, after his crabpots, to make sure none went adrift in yesterday's blow."

"Do they lose many in bad weather?"

"Yes, a lot."

They watched the sail idly as they sailed along, but she was too far away to distinguish, save that the sails were brown, like their own.

"I wonder if your dad got back last night," said Jack suddenly, after a pause.

"I say, I hadn't thought of it," said Tony. "I'm afraid he'll be worrying about us if he did. I'm sorry about that."

" Yes," said Jack. " We know we're safe but he doesn't. Perhaps he didn't get back after all. Anyway, he'll soon know we're safe now."

" He may know already," said Tony. " I expect they can see us from the cliff, if they were looking out, and if he's home I'm sure Dad will be," he added.

Half an hour passed. They were " fetching " the harbour on the starboard tack, while the brown-sailed boat, coming from the westward, was fetching it on the port tack, so that the boats were on converging courses.

" Look!" cried Jack, peering at the stranger under the foot of the mainsail as she drew nearer. " I believe it's the lifeboat."

" The lifeboat?" echoed Tony, bending down to look in his turn. " Why, so it is," he agreed, the bright red, white and blue of the stranger's hull being unmistakable. " There must have been a wreck. I wonder where it was."

As the boats converged, sundry members of the lifeboat's crew waved a greeting with oilskin-clad arms. The boys responded.

" Where's the wreck?" shouted Tony, as soon as they were within hailing distance.

" Wreck!" cried the coxswain, in mock indignation. " You're the only wreck we've heard of. We've been sailing around looking for ye all the night and here ye be safe and sound seemingly, praise the Lord. Where ye been?"

The boys looked at one another in astonishment.

So they had been the cause of the lifeboat's launch
and thirteen honest fishermen had lost a night's sleep
on their behalf. A lump rose in Tony's throat that he
had some difficulty in swallowing, but at last he managed
to reply.

"We were blown away in the gale. It took us all
night to get back."

The coxswain acknowledged the information with
an upward flourish of the arm, that gesture, so common
to the seaman, which means "All right. I understand."

The lifeboat's sails fluttered down as the harbour
mouth was reached, the oars straggled out and the
crew commenced to row her to the slipway.

"Here, catch this line!" called the bowman, standing, a coil of rope in hand, in the bows. "We'll give
you a tow in."

But the coxswain intervened.

"Nay," he said, "they've come through last night's
blow without any help. Let them finish the job properly, then none can say that the lifeboat had to fetch
'em back. They've done manfully, sure enough."

So, unassisted and under her own sail, the *Spray*,
with her young crew safe aboard her, sailed proudly
into the cove. A goodly number of the villagers, with
Major Bamford amongst them, stood on the end of
the stone breakwater and as the little craft passed gave
her three hearty cheers.

Tony and Jack waved and cheered in response,
again, to their surprise, feeling lumps in their throats

and a queer tingling about the eyes at the warmth of
their greeting.

Tom Pascoe was waiting for them at the *Spray's*
mooring with the dinghy.

" Glad to see you back," he said heartily. " Here,
jump in and I'll put you ashore. I'll come off after-
wards and put the *Spray* to rights, but I reckon you'll
be pretty well wore out."

" We're not so much tired as hungry," said Jack,
laughing. " We'll be glad enough to get ashore to breakfast."

Major Bamford had walked round and was waiting
for them on the slip at the builder's yard.

" Well, boys," he said, " you've given us all a nasty
fright and yourselves as well, I expect. The car is in
the road, so come along. Breakfast and bed are what
you need, or I'm mistaken. You can tell me all about it
later."

Old Bill Pascoe was there too, to add his congratu-
lations on their safe return.

" I watched you go out yesterday morning, Master
Tony, and I told ye not to go far. I thought I saw
ye sail away to the westward," he said.

" We did at first," admitted Tony. " And then we
turned round and went to Boldrington Bay."

" There now, that was it!" ejaculated the old man.
" I didn't see ye turn back and the lifeboat went the
wrong way on what I told them. That's how they
didn't find ye. Howsoever, all's well that ends well,
and I told ye, now didn't I, Master Tony, that the little

old *Spray* was a boat that would bring ye home?" he wound up, his bewhiskered face beaming with the pride of the master builder satisfied with the work of his hands and brain.

"She certainly did that all right. She's a lovely little vessel," said Tony, as he followed his father to the car.

.　　.　　.　　.　　.　　.　　.

Under the Major's orders they faithfully carried out the course of treatment that he had prescribed for them. After a hearty breakfast—and never had the bacon and eggs and coffee to which Jack had looked forward tasted better—they went to bed and were asleep almost as soon as their heads touched their pillows. Waking in the afternoon, they found themselves refreshed and none the worse for their night afloat. They got downstairs just in time to join the Major at afternoon tea, which was carried out on to the broad veranda, and during the meal were able to give a fuller account of their adventures than they had been able to do during their hurried breakfast. He listened to their recital with great interest.

"It was very peculiar behaviour on the part of the people in the steam yacht," he commented. "I cannot understand it. Do you think it was because they considered you were in no danger?"

"That's what I suggested, sir," said Jack, "but Tony said no."

"I'm sure it was not that, Dad," said Tony. "It was blowing jolly hard at the time and we were making

pretty heavy weather of it. The waves were really big.
Sometimes, in the troughs, we could only see the waves
on each side of us. I believe they were afraid to launch
a boat."

" Well," said his father, " it was very cowardly
behaviour and, whatever the reason, I simply cannot
understand it. Was she an English yacht? What flag
was she flying? Did you see her name?"

" No. She had no flags up and she was too far
away to make out her name, even if we had thought of
it—which we didn't. When she steamed away and
left us, it took us by surprise. I should know her again,
though—at least I think I should."

They spent the evening quietly. The weather had
fined away, the wind had died to the merest breeze
and, as the night fell, there was a chill in the air.

" I suspect that there is fog about," said Major
Bamford, as they took an after-dinner stroll through
the grounds of the Hall. " There's a dampish feel in
the air."

" I believe you are right, Dad," said Tony, whose
quick ears had caught a distant sound. " Listen!"

They stopped and listened and presently through
the quiet air came the deep-toned note of a foghorn.
It was the Bellows Point lighthouse sending out its
signal to warn passing shipping of the danger.

CHAPTER X

Wreckers' Bay

By the next morning the fog had spread inland and Barlash Hall was shrouded in the white vapour. Little could be seen from the windows of the breakfast-room, save a short stretch of lawn and the vague, shadowy outline of the tops of the trees beyond.

" I am going over to Dovermouth this morning," said Major Bamford. " Would you boys care to come?"

Tony and Jack looked at one another.

" Will you be long, Dad?"

" Yes. I'm afraid my business will take me some time. You would have to amuse yourselves."

" Then I don't think we will come, thanks, Dad."

The Major smiled.

" Well, I think you are wise," he said. " Wandering about the streets of a town is not a very interesting occupation, or ought not to be, for boys of your age. What will you do with yourselves? Go and sit aboard the *Spray* and give her another clean up? You may do that, if you like, but, mind, no getting under way unless this fog really clears. It may lift as the sun gets up, but don't go for a sail unless Bill Pascoe gives you permission. You've had one experience of what can happen in a fog. You got out of it very lightly, as you did out of the gale. You may not be as lucky another time."

"All right, Dad, I promise we won't," said Tony. "I thought we might perhaps go to see Tom Wallis, and Jack hasn't seen the caves yet."

"It seems to me he hasn't seen anything except the *Spray*," said his father, laughing. "Take care of yourselves and don't get into mischief."

Half an hour later the boys were climbing the steep ascent to the cliff. As they breasted the slope, the gulping roar of the foghorn on the lighthouse at Bellows Point became more audible.

"How far is it to the lighthouse?" asked Jack.

"About three miles by land," said Tony.

"I should rather like to see it," said Jack.

"We'll go there some time. It's jolly interesting, but it's no good going this morning, because they won't let you in when the foghorn is working."

"What a swiz! Hullo, how funny it looks!"

They had reached the edge of the down. The fog was very thick and the cliff, which at this point dropped almost sheer, appeared to be cut off some fifty feet below, giving the boys the impression that they were poised on the edge of a bottomless abyss.

"It does look funny, doesn't it?" said Tony. "Come along, let's go to the caves. We'll leave Tom Wallis till later."

Walking warily—for, though they could see the

immediate path easily enough, the shrouding mist imparted a sense of unreality and instinct counselled caution—the boys came, after a few minutes, to the fork where the path led down to the beach.

"There's the sea!" cried Jack, when they had descended for some distance.

The sea, or rather the foam of the waves where they curled over to break on the shore, was visible as an irregular white line. Two minutes later, with a whoop and a shout, the boys leapt down on to the sands and raced to the water's edge.

"Is this anywhere near where we ran ashore that day?" asked Jack.

"It's the same bay. It may be the very spot where we talked to Sam. I can't say for certain."

"Where are the caves?" asked Jack, looking round. On the beach the fog was very thick and even the foot of the cliff, a few yards away, was barely visible.

The entrance to the first of the caves, of which there were three, was quite close by. It was a slanting crack in the rock, about eight feet wide at the base and running up to nothing some fifteen feet above. A few yards inside, the entrance narrowed rapidly, so that there was barely foot room on the little strip of sand, and the slope of the walls was such that the boys could not walk upright, but had to place one hand on the lower wall for support as they moved along. After twenty feet or so of this, the passage, if such it could be called, suddenly ended in a huge cavern.

It was almost pitch dark, for though, looking back, the boys could see the walls of rock leading down the passage to the entrance, the light did not penetrate beyond them; and, looking into the cave, a velvet curtain of impenetrable blackness seemed to hang before them. Jack found it not a little eerie standing there in the darkness, with the " drip, drip " of invisible falling water sounding all around them.

" Wait a minute," said Tony. " I've brought an electric torch."

Taking the flash lamp from his pocket, he pressed the button and sent the narrow beam of light dancing round the walls of the cave.

It was like a huge circular hall, sixty feet or more in diameter at the floor, with the walls mounting up into a tall dome-shaped roof so high in the centre that the rays from the torch failed to reach it.

" They say these caves were used by the smugglers in the old days," said Tony. " There's a hole up there that looks like the entrance to a passage," he added, directing the beam of his torch to where a dark patch showed in the rock face some fifty feet above their heads.

" Wouldn't it be fun to explore it?" said Jack. " I'd love to."

" I've thought of that," said Tony; " but the rock is almost sheer. You couldn't possibly climb up, and it would be such an awful job to bring ladders long enough to reach."

" Does the sea come into the cave?" asked Jack.

" Only just inside. The floor slopes up, as you can see, and this side is quite dry."

" I wonder if the smugglers had fights here with the preventive men," said Jack. " Two men could easily hold this place against a crowd. The entrance is so narrow and awkward the attackers would be at a terrible disadvantage and, besides, they wouldn't be able to see in, while, silhouetted against the light, they would show up to the defenders quite plainly."

" That's true," said Tony. " I dare say, if this cave could speak, it would have some wonderful tales to tell of all it has seen. Some pretty exciting and some pretty horrible too, I dare say, for Dad says that most of the smugglers were really bad men and some of them were frightfully cruel."

" I suppose they must have been," said Jack thoughtfully. " Tales in books so often make them almost into heroes, but I suppose they were really gangsters of olden days. If they were anything like the present-day ones, they must have been horrible enough, goodness knows."

" Ugh!" said Tony, " I should say so. Come on, let's see the other caves before this battery is all used up. I thought it was a fresh one, but it doesn't seem to be."

Snapping off the light, he led the way out on to the beach again. The fog showed no signs of clearing and drove along in billowy clouds of white vapour.

" This isn't like a London fog. There's as much difference as milk and treacle," said Jack.

The entrances to the other caves were at the farther end of the beach, nearly a quarter of a mile away. They were side by side, in the form of almost perfect arches.

" They look like a big letter B, lying on its flat side," said Jack.

" So they do," agreed Tony. " I've never noticed it before. Perhaps it's the fog makes it more obvious. We'll explore this one first; come on."

With Tony in the lead, the boys entered the first archway. The sandy floor was smooth and wide and, as Jack said, there was room for a baby car to drive up it. It ran straight into the cliff for about thirty yards.

" That leads into the other cave," said Tony, pointing to a narrow passage-like opening in the left-hand wall. " Mind your head," he added a moment later. " The roof gets low here for a little way, but it isn't far."

Crouching down, the boys stumbled forward through the loose sand.

" What's that?" said Jack suddenly, in a whisper.

The tinkle of something falling from a height, striking and bouncing down the rocky side of the cave, sounded from farther ahead.

The boys stopped dead and listened.

" It's probably a stalactite falling," said Tony, after a pause.

" That wasn't a stalactite," said Jack, " it was metal. I could tell by the sound."

For a few moments the boys stood listening, but could hear nothing further.

"Oh, well," said Tony, "it's probably somebody in the cave."

"Who?" whispered Jack.

"How should I know?" demanded Tony. "It's probably somebody exploring like ourselves. A visitor, I expect. There are several staying in the village. It's not the ghost of a smuggler, anyway."

Switching on his torch, he advanced into the cave. Another few feet forward and the roof began to slope upwards and he could stand upright. The cave opened out and became a wide corridor, whose walls towered upwards into the gloom.

"There's no one here," said Tony, as he flashed his lamp around.

The beam of light glinted on something half buried in the sand. He bent forward and picked it up.

"Whatever's this?" he said, in a puzzled voice.

By the light of the lamp the boys examined their find. It proved to be a pair of oddly shaped pieces of metal, attached to each other by straps. They were shaped something like a horseman's spur, but narrower. One arm was straighter than the other and was flattened to a width of almost three inches, while its fellow was curved and springy. The actual spur, where the rowel would have been in an ordinary spur, was a blunt, round spike about two inches in length.

"What funny things," said Tony. "I wonder what they are for."

" I wonder where they came from," said Jack, looking up. " They're the things that we heard fall."

Tony directed the beam of his lamp aloft. It was growing feeble, for the battery was running out, but in its dim ray the precipitous walls could be seen running up almost sheer, on either side, to meet the roof nearly fifty feet above. There was no explanation of the mystery there.

" It may have been left by the long-ago smugglers," suggested Tony. " Whatever was holding it has rusted or rotted away and let it fall. They say there were all sorts of secret passages and iron ladders in places, but they've all gone now."

Jack shook his head.

" The smugglers didn't leave these, I'm sure," he said. " Look at the leather, that's new; and they are made of rustless steel. This is modern stuff. It can't have been made very long ago."

" That's true," admitted Tony. " I was an ass not to see it."

" How much farther does this cave go in?"

" Not far. Just a few feet round a corner. That's a bit farther than we can see."

" Is anyone there?" said Jack.

Unconsciously the boys had been speaking in whispers. They looked at one another.

Side by side they moved forward, the rays of the lamp lighting up the cave ahead of them. They reached the turn, rounded it, and the lamp's rays reflected on the end wall of the cave.

" There's no one here, anyway," said Tony.

At that moment they heard a sound behind them in the cave. Quickly they moved to the corner and looked back. A bright light was shining from a ledge high up close to the roof.

The ledge was not to be distinguished from the roof itself by anyone looking up from the floor of the cave, and only the light above it threw it into relief. The boys watched in a fascinated silence as a man suddenly swung himself over the edge and commenced to climb down the precipitous rock face.

" How on earth——" began Jack, in a whisper.

" Hush!" hissed Tony, laying a warning hand on Jack's arm and switching off his torch.

Slowly the man climbed down and reached the floor of the cave. He directed the rays of his torch on the ground, evidently searching for something. The boys could hear him muttering to himself. He made his area of search wider and at last stood up, obviously puzzled; then he sent his light flickering up the sides of the cavern, evidently looking to see if the object of his search had lodged in some crack or crevice of the rock.

Again he swung his light round, aiming it directly at the boys, who shrank quickly back behind the projecting corner. Had he seen them? The light remained pointed in their direction for several seconds while they stood with beating hearts, listening for his approaching footsteps on the sands, but at last, after some moments of suspense, the light was withdrawn.

With a sigh of relief, the boys relaxed after the tension and then plucked up courage to peep once more.

The man was preparing to ascend the side of the cave. He adjusted his lamp to give out a diffused light that was not concentrated in a single beam, and slung it round his neck so that it rested on his chest. Then he commenced to climb.

Slowly but surely he rose. Growing bolder, as the man concentrated on his task, and knowing that, being outside the radius of his light, they would be invisible in the darkness, the boys crept cautiously forward.

In each hand the stranger held something like a short bar and seemed to feel about with it before getting a hold. In the same way he fumbled, even more, with his feet, before trusting his weight on one in making a step.

"I see how he does it," whispered Tony, in an eager voice.

"Hush!" hissed Jack, in his turn, but the man was fully occupied and had heard nothing.

They watched him climb higher and higher. He reached the ledge and, as his hand stretched over the edge, they heard a slight tinkle as of a piece of metal dropping on rock. A moment later he had swung himself on to the ledge and disappeared from sight. The rays of the light showed above the ledge for a few moments and then quickly faded, as though the lamp had been carried away.

" I wonder who he is and what he wanted," said Jack.

" I can guess what he wanted—those spur things—but who he is I've no idea," said Tony. " It's jolly queer, that's all I know."

They approached the spot where the man had commenced his climb. By the dying light of their lamp they could see a series of holes drilled into the face of the rock, zig-zagging upwards about a foot apart.

" Where are those things we found?" said Tony.

Jack, who was carrying them, handed them to him.

" Let me try. Do they fit the holes?"

He tried the blunt spikes in the holes. They slipped in perfectly.

" I see," he said.

" It's more than I do," said Jack.

" Come outside on the beach," said Tony. " He might come back and see us. We can't talk here."

CHAPTER XI

The Passage in the Cave

"These things are like climbing irons, only for rock instead of trees," said Tony, a few minutes later, when, safe on the open beach, they stopped to discuss the situation.

"Look!" Squatting down on the sand, he leaned his back against the cliff. "You fit the flat part under your foot," he went on, suiting his action to his words, "then the rounded part curves up over your toes and the strap fastens behind the heel and holds it in place."

"I see," said Jack, as Tony stood up with an iron in position on his foot. "And the spur thing sticks out in front, like an extra big toe. Of course, this fellow has made it easier by boring holes to take the spur in the rocks itself."

"That's right," said Tony. "He'd need holes here, for not the best climbing irons in the world would help him up the wall of the cave. It's too sheer and smooth."

"I wonder what he threw the climbing irons down for," said Jack.

"Don't be an ass," said Tony. "He didn't throw them down on purpose. He dropped them by accident.

I expect he'd been down on the beach for something before we came along and had climbed up to the ledge. Once there, I don't suppose he needs irons any more, so he took them off and then accidentally dropped them."

"Why didn't he come down after them right away, then?" asked Jack. "It was some time before he came."

"Because," said Tony, "I expect he'd have to go and fetch another pair from somewhere. He evidently doesn't keep any spares on the ledge and, while he was away fetching them, we came along and picked up this lot. They'd be jolly awkward to walk in," he wound up, taking a few halting steps forward. "The spur catches in the ground if you don't look out. You have to lift your feet."

"Couldn't we climb up to the ledge this afternoon?" said Jack. "I'd love to explore and see what there is up there."

"We will," said Tony. "We can easily get two bars of iron to do for the hand grips. If we get them the right diameter, that is all that matters."

"I know," said Jack. "Just a couple of short bolts of the right size. The thread on the end would help to stop them from coming out."

"So it would," agreed Tony.

He bent down and took the iron off his foot.

"We'd better be getting home," he said. "It must be nearly lunch time."

The fog showed no sign of lifting and continued to

blow steadily in from seaward as they retraced their
steps homewards. At the little ironmonger's shop,
on the corner in the village, they were able to procure
two bolts about six inches long, which Jack affirmed
would be ideal for the hand grips.

" Shall you tell your father?" he asked, as they neared
the Hall.

" I was just thinking of that," said Tony. " I'm
afraid he may stop us going, but I think we'd better.
I hate to do anything behind his back. He's such a
good sport."

" I know," agreed Jack. " I think you're right.
My dad always tells me not to deceive him about
anything. He says if he can trust my word, he will
always be able to take my version and back me up
if I get into a scrape, but, if I told him lies and he found
me out, he'd never know whether to believe me or the
other fellow."

" Yes," said Tony. " I think he's right, too. We'll
tell Dad. I'd rather."

However, they had no chance to tell Major Bamford,
for when they reached the Hall the housekeeper greeted
them with the news that he had rung up to say that
he was detained at Dovermouth and would not be
back to lunch; so, after partaking of that meal, the boys
armed themselves with two pocket torches—making
sure that the batteries were in good condition—and the
climbing irons and returned to the beach.

When they re-entered the cave, a tremor of un-
certainty crept over them. The caves were open to

the public, so they were not trespassing on anyone's private property, but somehow they could not help a certain feeling of nervousness. They flashed their torches into every nook and cranny to make certain that the cave was empty and that there was no sign of life on the ledge above.

" We needn't funk it," said Tony. " We've as much right here as anyone else."

" I know," said Jack. " Who is funking it?"

Both the boys laughed.

" Oh, well," said Tony, " which of us is going up first?"

" Toss for it," said Jack, producing a coin and sending it spinning into the air.

" Heads!" cried Tony.

" Heads it is," said Jack, retrieving the coin.

" Right," said Tony. " I go."

Squatting down on the sand, he adjusted the irons on his feet.

" They do feel queer," he said, as he stood up. " Now for it."

He approached the wall of the cave and, slipping the spur on his foot into the hole, he shipped the hand grip in another, higher up, and hauled himself upwards. He fumbled a good deal in making the next step.

" There must be a knack in this," he said. " The holes are a bit far apart. I suppose the man who bored them wasn't allowing for people as short in the leg as we are. I think I can just manage."

"I expect he didn't want to bore any more holes than he need," suggested Jack.

Laboriously, Tony raised himself another three holes.

"Be careful," advised Jack. "Mind you don't slip. You look like a fly on a wall."

"Oh, I'm safe enough," said Tony. "These clips give a splendid foothold and the bars are quite good to hold on to with your hands. You've just got to be careful to keep the strain pulling down, so that they can't slip out. Dash it."

There was a tinkle of iron on rock and something fell at Jack's feet.

It was one of the hand grips that Tony had accidentally let fall.

"Here you are, catch," said Jack, picking it up and tossing it to his chum. At the second attempt Tony caught it with his disengaged hand and then, to his chum's astonishment, started to climb down again.

"Hullo, what's the matter?" cried Jack.

"I'm coming down," said Tony, and a few moments later he stood on the sandy floor of the cave.

"That was a jolly lucky escape," he said. "With only one hand grip, I was helpless. I couldn't move. I could only hang on. If I'd got nearly to the top and then dropped it, I should have been properly treed, for you could hardly have thrown it straight enough for me to catch at that height—with only one hand too. I don't know what I should have done."

"Whew!" whistled Jack. "I never thought of that.

Well, what about it?" he added, after a few moments'
pause. " Do we give it up?"

" No fear," said Tony. " I'm only getting my wind.
It's pretty stiff work, when you're not used to it anyway. I'm going to tie the grips to my wrists with
string."

" Jolly good wheeze!" cried Jack. " I've got a fine
bit of stuff in my pocket. Marline, off the *Spray*.
Here you are."

It did not take the boys long to fix loops to the
grips and, with these securely slipped over his wrists,
Tony again essayed the climb. This time he got on
more quickly and was soon twenty feet above Jack's
head. Here another unforeseen check occurred.

" I can't see the holes," he panted. " The light
from your torch isn't strong enough to show them up
now. I want another hand to hold my torch."

" Hold it in your mouth," advised Jack.

Holding on with one hand, Tony fumbled in his
pocket with the other and finally got his torch alight.
Then he gripped it in his teeth and recommenced his
ascent. Jack watched him anxiously. At last he reached
his goal and disappeared on to the ledge.

" There's tons of room up here," he called down,
poking his head over the edge a moment later. " This
shelf must be quite eight feet wide and there's a
passage of some sort opening off it. Wait a jiffy and
I'll throw the irons down to you. Stand from
under."

One by one he dropped the irons, and they fell with

soft thuds in the sand. Jack picked them up and fixed them in position.

" I'm coming up!" he called.

Jack was not quite as tall as Tony, so he found the ascent even more difficult. The holes were just a little too far apart for him to reach easily and the little extra distance made all the difference. Every step upwards entailed a stretch and a strain, but he climbed steadily, with his torch gripped tightly in his teeth. At last he felt Tony's hand grasp his wrist, and a moment later he rolled over the edge of the ledge and lay puffing and blowing to get back his breath.

When he sat up he was able to take stock of his surroundings. The ledge on which they lay formed a platform about twenty feet long and a good eight feet in width at its widest part, tapering to nothing at the ends. In the middle, against the wall of the cave, it was possible for a man to stand upright, but it sloped upwards towards the outer edge, which was only some four feet below the roof. Near the middle was a dark opening which appeared to be the beginning of a passage.

" Get the irons off," said Tony. " We'll leave them here, ready for us when we come back. There," he added, when he had placed them in a crevice in the rock. " Now we shall know where to find them and we shan't be able to drop them and lose them in the passage."

Flashing their torches ahead of them, the boys entered the passage. It was about three feet wide and something over five feet high and evidently ran through the solid rock. The walls and floor were comparatively dry, but a steady draught of damp air blew in their faces.

"The other end must be open," said Jack. "This wind is blowing from somewhere, but it's fearfully damp and wettish."

"That'll be the fog," said Tony.

For some distance the passage ran straight and then began to curve gradually to the left.

"It's pretty long," said Jack. "We must have come a good hundred yards already, I should think. I wonder how much farther it goes."

"There must be an end somewhere," said Tony, who was in the lead. "Hullo, look here. There's a fork to the left. Now," he added, as he stood at the junction, shining his lamp up each passage in turn, "which shall we take?"

There seemed little to choose between the two.

"When in doubt, choose the right path," quoted Jack sententiously.

"Yes," said Tony, laughing, "but how do we know the right path is the right one?"

"We don't," said Jack, "but we can go along it and find out. Anyway, the wind is coming out of the right-hand passage, so let's try that one first."

The decision thus made, they moved on again. The passage continued as before, the floor, of rough rock, being worn comparatively smooth in the middle as though by the passage of many feet. It kept a uniform width, but in some places was higher than in others, and while a man of average height would have had to stoop most of the time, the boys could walk upright. On and on they went. The way seemed interminable.

" Look out! Stop!" cried Tony at last. A couple of yards ahead their torches shone on a blank void.

Dropping down on their hands and knees, the boys cautiously approached the edge. The passage ended abruptly in a sheer drop into a dark abyss. About two feet from the end a stout iron bar had been firmly cemented into the floor.

" This looks as though it might be another of their patent staircases," said Tony. " Hold my legs. I'm going to have a good look."

Lying down flat on his face, he wormed his way forward until his head and shoulders projected over the abyss. Jack squatted on his legs, gripping them with his knees and keeping a firm hold on the iron bar.

" Yes," Tony reported. " There are holes bored in the rock here too, like the other cave. I know," he almost shouted suddenly. " Give me your torch, Jack."

Holding them both below him at arm's length, he peered intently downwards.

" Yes," he said. " I do believe it's the cave. You know, the first one we explored this morning. The distance would be about right. We're in the hole near the roof that I pointed out to you. Get off my legs."

With Jack keeping a careful grip on him, he wriggled back into a sitting position.

" That's that," he said. " Now for the other passage."

" The right passage was the wrong one in this case," said Jack, laughing, as they retraced their steps.

" Yes," said Tony, " there are times when left is right. Here we are at the turn."

" Hullo," said Jack, after they proceeded for a few yards. " This passage is different. It's not rock any more, but brick."

" So it is," agreed Tony, stopping. " Yes, this part has been built. Look at the walls," he added, flashing his light around.

The moss-grown walls, discoloured with age, were indeed of brick, as was also the domed roof. Although obviously very old, there were signs that the passage had been frequently used of late and it needed no trained scout to trace the marks on the floor. The passage was higher, too—a clear six feet to the middle of the arch. It did not run straight, but in a series of wandering zig-zags, so that it was impossible for them to see more than a few yards ahead.

After their pause, the boys moved steadily forward, ears on the alert for any sound, but all was silent.

" I say," said Jack at last, " will this passage never end? We seem to have been walking for ages. How far do you think we've come?"

" I've no idea," said Tony. " We'll count our steps going back and time ourselves, then we'll be able to make a rough calculation. Do you notice there's no wind now?"

" Yes," agreed Jack. " I suppose the wind came from the other cave. This end must be closed up, for, as you say, the air is quite still. It feels drier, too. Hullo!"

The end was in sight. The passage suddenly sloped slightly upwards and ended in a flight of steps, while, at the foot of the steps, on the left, was a stout oaken door, which stood slightly ajar. Pushing it open, the boys entered a small cave-like room with an old iron-bound chest against one wall.

" Whew!" whistled Jack. " This looks interesting."

He stepped forward and tried to raise the lid.

" It's locked, I expect," said Tony, pointing to the huge padlock.

Jack gave it a sharp tug.

" It is," he said. " There's nothing else here," he added, looking round. " Let's try the stairs."

At the top of the flight of steps was an old door almost black with age. Putting his ear to the door, Jack listened for a few moments, then shook his head to signify that he could hear nothing.

The door was fastened with a cumbrous mechanism of iron. It, too, looked old, but was freshly oiled and was evidently in good working condition.

" Look here," said Tony.

He had discovered a flap, which, when raised, disclosed a small hole, evidently for use as a spy hole, but too high for him to reach.

" Give me a leg up," he said.

Jack dropped on one knee and Tony used the other as a stool, which brought his eye on a level with the hole. Lifting the flap again, he peered through and a moment later turned a startled face on his companion.

" I say," he whispered, " we're in a house somewhere. There's a lovely old room inside. All oak panelled."

" Is anyone there?"

" I can't see anyone," said Tony, after again applying his eye to the hole, " but I can't see all the room. It's ever so quaint. I wonder where it can be."

" Let me have a look," said Jack.

The boys changed places.

" Shall we go inside?" suggested Jack, as he stepped down.

The boys looked at one another.

" I wonder how you get the door open," said Tony, shining his torch on the mechanism.

Jack studied it closely for a minute.

" I see," he said. " It's quite simple. You just lift this knob. The rest of the gear is evidently for opening the door from the other side. It's probably a secret door, and is disguised as part of the wall of the room."

He lifted the knob and pulled. The door swivelled easily and swung open without a sound. Jack stepped cautiously through the opening.

No sooner was he through than he leaped backwards, almost knocking down Tony, who was close behind him. Without a word, he pushed the door back into place.

" What's up?" demanded Tony, in a whisper.

" There's a man inside there," Jack whispered back. " He's sitting at a table at the far end, with a lot of papers and little packets on it."

" Did he see you?"

" I don't think so. He seemed intent on whatever he was doing, but he may have heard us. Give me a leg up and I'll peep."

Tony knelt, and Jack, stepping up on his knee, lifted the flap. He was down again in a moment.

" He's walking towards the door," he said, in a tense whisper.

CHAPTER XII

Trapped

" Come on. Quick."

Turning, Tony and Jack scurried down the steps and fled along the passage at their top speed. It was lucky they were both wearing rubber-soled shoes, which made their escape as noiseless as possible, for, in their momentary panic, their one idea was to put as much distance as possible between themselves and the door before it opened, and, had they been leather shod, the sound of their footsteps on the brick floor would have resounded down the passage.

They continued their headlong flight for a good hundred yards, and then, as if by mutual consent, stopped to listen for sounds of pursuit.

The windings of the passage made it impossible for them to see far, and, while this had the advantage of hiding them from a possible pursuer, it also made it possible for a pursuer, if he trod quietly and did not shine his torch ahead, to get within twenty-five yards or so of them without giving warning of his approach.

" Is he coming, do you think?" asked Jack, in a tense whisper.

Tony shrugged his shoulders.

" Put your torch out," he whispered back.

They had shrouded their torches by putting their hands over the bulbs and letting just sufficient light filter between their fingers for them to see their way. Standing in complete darkness, they would be able to see the glow of any approaching light before its carrier reached the bend. Side by side they waited in silence.

Suddenly the stillness was broken by a distant clang.

" What's that? Is it the door?" whispered Jack.

" No. The mechanism of the door is so good that it opens and shuts without a sound. It would be impossible to bang it. It must be the door of that little room— or no, I know what it is. He's been to that chest we saw in the room and he's let the lid drop with a bang."

Jack breathed a sigh of relief.

" Good. That means he didn't see us after all and wasn't chasing us. Come on, let's get out of here. I've had enough excitement for one afternoon."

" So have I," agreed Tony, switching on his torch and leading the way down the passage. " We'll tell Dad about this to-night. There's something very funny going on. I wonder what it all means. It seems very fishy to me."

They reached the ledge above the cave without further incident. As they did so, Tony gave a cry of dismay.

" We're trapped!" he cried. " At least one of us is," he added.

"Why?" demanded Jack, retrieving the climbing irons from where they had left them. "Here are the irons. We're all right."

"No we're not," insisted Tony. "There are two of us and only one lot of irons. We got up all right because it was easy for me to throw the things down to you, but will whoever goes down first be able to throw them up again? We ought to have thought of that, especially after I dropped one. We ought to have brought a length of string, then we could have pulled them up as we liked easily enough."

"We'll chuck them up all right," said Jack, with a confidence he did not feel. "Go on. You go first."

"No, you," said Tony.

"You led the way up, so you ought to lead the way down," objected Jack.

Tony laughed a little ruefully.

"I see what it is," he said. "We both think the one left behind is likely to be treed. I suppose we'll have to toss for it."

He spun a coin in the air.

"Heads," called Jack.

By the light of their torches, the boys saw that the coin lay head uppermost.

"Now," said Jack, "you go."

"No fear," objected Tony, "you won, so you go."

"I won," agreed Jack, "so I can choose what I do. I say you are to go."

For answer Tony balanced the coin again on his thumb and finger.

" I'll toss again," he said. " This time the winner goes and no arguing about it. Do you agree?"

" All right," said Jack, with a laugh. " Tails."

" It's heads," he cried, a moment later. " You go after all."

" All right, I'll go," said Tony slowly, " but it isn't fair all the same."

Adjusting the irons and taking his torch in his teeth, he lowered himself cautiously over the edge of the ledge, and slowly and carefully made the descent. Once safe on the floor of the cave, he took off the irons.

" Now," he called. " Stand back and shine your light so that it shows up the edge of the ledge."

He selected the first iron and, standing back, took careful aim. It was a beautiful shot. The iron rose through the air and landed at the top of its flight almost noiselessly on the ledge.

" Got him," cried Jack, in surprised triumph.

Tony picked up one of the iron bolts and made another shot. It hit the wall of the cave just below the ledge and fell back. A second attempt did the same, the third attempt hit the roof, and half a dozen more attempts ended in failure.

" If at first you don't succeed, try, try, try again," mocked Jack, popping his head over the edge of the ledge. " Take a rest, old chap, and throw steady. I shall be up here all night at this rate."

Tony took his advice and waited for a few moments, then he made another attempt. The iron sailed high into the air towards the ledge.

" Got it?" he cried.

" No," came the surprising reply. " It's not on the ledge."

" Where is it then?" cried Tony. " It didn't fall back again. I'm sure of that."

Jack lay down and peered over the edge.

" Switch your light out," he called. " It blinds me."

When Tony's light was extinguished, he carefully searched the wall of the cave with his torch.

" I see it," he cried. " It's in a crevice of the rock just below here."

" Can you reach it?"

" Reach it? Not a hope. It's a good nine feet away."

" Whew!" whistled his friend. " That's made a mess of things. Now, what are we going to do?"

" There's only one thing to do," said Jack. " You must go and get some twine, see you have enough, you'd better bring at least sixty feet, and get another bolt. It's lucky it is only a bolt that is stuck. If it had been one of the irons, I'd have been properly trapped. You'll have to climb up to me with the cord."

Tony thought for a moment.

" Right, old man," he called. " It's the only way. I'll leave the iron here and take the bolt for a pattern. Cheerio. Keep your tail up. I won't be long."

So saying, he left the cave and set off at a steady trot along the sands in the direction of the village.

.   .   .   .

Left to himself, Jack calculated that it would be at

least an hour before Tony could possibly get back
with the twine. It would be a long wait. In order to
conserve the power, he switched off his torch and sat in
the darkness, listening to the faint murmur of the
waves breaking on the beach outside. There was
plenty to occupy his thoughts. What was the fellow
up to in the house at the end of the passage? Why
was he using the passage, and what was the stuff stowed
away in the iron-bound chest? It was something fishy,
of course, but what? Could he be a smuggler? Jack
knew that it was still worth while to cheat the customs;
the only drawback was the difficulty of getting away
with it without being caught. He racked his brains.
From time to time he consulted his wrist watch with
his torch. An hour had passed, and he was momentarily
expecting Tony to return at any moment, when the
sound of distant footsteps broke the stillness.

At first he thought succour was at hand, but a moment
later he realized that it was not Tony, for Tony's
footsteps would not ring and echo on the sandy floor
of the cave, as these did. It was someone approaching
down the passage.

A thrill of dismay swept over him, for he felt that he
could scarcely hope to escape discovery. He knew, of
course, that he had a perfect right to be where he was.
He was no trespasser, but, somehow, that thought did
not console him. The fact that he was sure the man was
up to no good rather shook his confidence.

He crawled quietly to the end of the ledge and,
pressing himself into the angle where the roof met the

floor, lay flat, taking care that his hands and face, which might have given him away by showing as white patches in the darkness, were well hidden.

Then the absurdity of this precaution struck him, and he almost laughed aloud in spite of his anxiety. It was useless to hide his hands and face when he exposed the broadest part of his white flannel shorts in full view. No. He must take his chance. If the man shone his torch his way, he was certain to be discovered. He quickly changed his plan. He rolled over into a sitting position, and let his legs dangle over the edge of the ledge.

The footsteps drew rapidly nearer and suddenly a man appeared in the mouth of the passage. He had already hung his light round his neck and, seating himself on a projecting piece of rock, he began to adjust his climbing irons.

Jack watched him, fascinated, scarcely daring to breathe.

The man finished his task and, crawling forward, quite unconscious of Jack's presence, swung himself over the edge of the ledge. His head had almost disappeared from sight when Jack, thinking to escape detection, cautiously lifted his legs on to the ledge. Although soundless, so far as he knew, the movement was his undoing, for it attracted the man's attention. He gave a startled exclamation, and quickly clambered back on to the ledge again.

" Who's there?" he demanded, in a menacing voice.

" It's me," said Jack, trying to speak nonchalantly.

The beam of the man's torch shone in his face, blinding him to all else.

"What are you doing here? How did you get here?" asked the man, evidently puzzled, but reassured to find that he had only a boy to deal with.

"I climbed up," said Jack.

"You climbed up," echoed the man. "Impossible. How?"

"I found some funny iron things down there," said Jack, pointing downwards. "I found they fitted on to my shoes, and then I noticed the holes in the rock, and here I am."

"Yes," said the man slowly. "Here you are. And what do you propose to do now?"

"Well," said Jack. "I'd like to get down again, but I've dropped one of the climbing irons and I'm stuck. Will you help me to get down, please?"

"Help you to get down," repeated the man, smiling evilly. "Yes, I think I will."

He came towards the boy and, seizing him by the arm, dragged him towards the centre of the ledge where there was more room.

"Little boys who poke their noses where they have no business and are not wanted are better out of the way."

He forced Jack back to the edge.

"Your friends will think you fell," he went on, still with the evil smile playing about his lips. "Well, they will be right. Ah! What's that?"

A shaft of light showed through the tunnel on the

floor of the cave, and a moment later Tony's cheery voice could be heard vigorously singing:

" We've been a long time coming, but we're on the way."

With a muffled curse, the man gripped Jack to him, stifled his shout for help with a muzzling hand, and dragged him, struggling and fighting, to the passage. Just before it was too late, Jack remembered the climbing iron which he still held in his hand and, though almost helpless in the man's powerful grip, with a despairing effort he managed to toss the iron over the edge of the ledge on to the sandy floor below.

CHAPTER XIII

Sam to the Rescue

When Tony left Jack on the ledge, he hurried out of the cave and along the shore at his top speed, concern for the safety of his chum lending wings to his feet. He arrived at the top of the cliff, after the steep climb up its face, panting and breathless, but, after stumbling along for a few yards, again managed to break into a trot which grew faster when he reached a favourable gradient.

He kept up his steady run until he reached the village and, having obtained a duplicate bolt and a large ball of string, which the shopman assured him was fully a hundred feet in length, he wasted no time in setting off on his return journey.

As he reached the cliff top above the path, he was startled to hear the double whistle, which he recognized as the same that he and Jack had heard on the second day of their holidays, on the beach below. Instinctively he stopped dead, but the thought of Jack, still on the ledge, made his hesitation merely a momentary one. Hurrying down the cliff path, he arrived safely on the beach and peered cautiously into the fog.

It was still as thick as ever—a real sea fog, and not

even the heat of the summer afternoon sun had done more than thin it a little.

Tony kept close to the foot of the cliff and, moving on warily, kept a sharp lookout. He had passed the mouth of the first cave, and was nearly half-way to his goal, when he caught sight of the shadowy form of a man standing on the sands between the cliff and the water.

Again Tony stopped dead. As he did so the man put his fingers to his lips, and again the double whistle rang out.

Who was this man? Was he in league with the smugglers—if smugglers they were—in the cave? In any case, whoever the stranger was, Jack must be reached. Keeping an anxious eye on the man, and trusting that, in the fog and against the dark background of the cliff, he would not be noticed, Tony moved cautiously forward, step by step. He had drawn level and was almost past when the stranger spoke.

" Oh, there ye be," he said, striding towards Tony. " I was wondering what had become of ye."

Tony's first shock of apprehension at being discovered quickly changed to a wave of relief. To his surprise, he recognized the voice of the stranger as that of his fisherman friend, young Sam Tonkin.

" Why, Sam!" he cried. " How did you know I was coming? Have you seen Jack? or," he added, as Sam came close enough for him to see his face, " did you think I was somebody else?"

" Well," said Sam, " I didn't think you was you,

that's sure. I did think you was somebody else. What be you doing down here all alone?"

Without hesitation, Tony took Sam into his confidence, quickly outlining their day's adventure: how they had climbed to the ledge in the cave, how they had explored the passage and found the little room and the flight of steps, and the door which gave entry into what was evidently a large house. How he and Jack had fled, thinking they had been seen, and how his chum had had to be left treed on the ledge while he fetched the string to rescue him.

As he listened to Tony's story, the young fisherman's face grew grave.

" So that's how he got down to the beach," he muttered half to himself. " I wondered how he done it. Gran'fer has waited up top for him to come up the path, when he've thought I was a meeting him down here, but he've never seen a sign of him.

" But your friend's still up on that there ledge," he went on, seeming to awake from his thoughts. " We must get him down and quick too. If the man you saw is the man I think he is, and he catches your friend up there, there's no saying what he mightn't do to him. Him and his friends are queer customers, and liable to turn rough if they'm crossed."

" Who are they and what are they doing?" asked Tony, hurrying after the young fisherman, who led the way to the cave with long strides.

" No time to tell you now. We can talk of that by and by when your friend's safe."

As they entered the cave, thinking to cheer Jack up and give him warning of their approach, Tony broke into song. As we know, Jack heard the song, and though he was powerless to answer it, it came in the nick of time to save him from being hurled from the ledge.

"Jack!" cried Tony, looking upwards. "Jack, are you there?"

There was no answer. When the echo of his shouts died away, the cave, save for the murmur of the waves on the beach outside, was as silent as the grave. The simile flashed into Tony's mind and sent a shudder of apprehension for his friend through him.

"That's funny," he said. "I wonder what can have happened to him. Jack! Jack!" he hailed again loudly. "Are you there?"

Again there was no answer.

"Where's that climbing gear?" demanded Sam suddenly, his voice tense.

"I left one iron here," said Tony, flashing his lamp to the side of the cave where the iron lay. "There it is, but Jack has the other. I threw it up to him."

"Then we're euchred," said Sam. "If what you told me is right, we can't get up with only one iron."

"Jack!"

Desperate at Sam's words, of which he realized the truth, Tony shouted again, stepping back to look up as he did so.

"Hullo!" he ejaculated. "What's that?"

As he stepped back he had trodden on something, which the light of his torch revealed to be the missing climbing iron.

" How did this get here?" cried Tony in surprise.

Ignoring the question, Sam picked it up and, sitting down on the sands, quickly adjusted the irons on his feet.

" Look," he said earnestly as he stood up, slipping the loops of the bolts over his wrists. " I'm going up after your friend. There may have been some funny work up there, and I'm going to find out. I'll tell you this much. I've been meeting a man on the beach and handing over the stuff what I had from the steam yacht, or her launch, time and again, but I've never seen where he went to. It's always been at night time, except, like to-day, when there's fog about. There's only one way up from this beach that I know of, but I never thought of the caves, for we all believed there was no way out of them except on to the beach."

" What stuff do you mean?" asked Tony, as Sam prepared to climb.

" French stuff of some sort," said Sam. " The man said 'tis since the tariff was put on. The way he showed it, tariffs ain't fair. Anyway, what I done was only free tradin', same as they used to do along here in the olden day. The fishin's been that rotten a fellow can't make a living. I had to do something."

" Does he pay you well?" asked Tony.

" Five pounds a trip," said Sam, setting his iron-shod toe in the first hole. " 'Tis better than fishing, but we mustn't waste time talking. You'll have to let me have your lamp."

Taking Tony's lamp in his teeth, he commenced to climb. With his extra length of leg, he could negotiate the distance between the holes more easily than the boys had done, and in a very short time he reached the ledge and disappeared over the edge.

" There's a lamp here with the bulb broke. That's all," he called down a moment later. " So long."

" Wait," called Tony. " Throw the irons down. I'll come with you."

" Nay," said Sam. " You stay below. I can do all that's needed up here. If I don't come back in an hour, you go for the police, but we don't want them in it unless it can't be helped. So long," he added again.

" You turn left at the fork," shouted Tony, as the light of his torch faded.

Sam entered the passage and, shining Tony's torch ahead of him, walked forward, pausing at intervals to listen. He reached the junction of the roads and took the left fork as Tony had instructed.

Cautiously making his way onwards, he came at length to the entrance to the little room at the foot of the steps which Tony had described.

The door was closed. Sam listened a moment and then tried the handle. It was locked. Turning away, he ascended the steps, again pausing outside the upper door to listen. He thought he could distinguish the faint murmur of voices on the farther side. He looked for the spy hole, of which Tony had told him. Carefully lifting the flap, he peeped through into the room beyond.

Two men were seated at a table, while in front of them stood a boy, whom he knew to be Jack, guarded by a third man whose swarthy features he immediately recognized as the one with whom he kept rendezvous on the beach below.

Jack was speaking.

" I tell you I don't know anything. I just came into the cave by chance. I saw the irons in the sand and the holes in the wall. I thought I'd climb up to explore, then I dropped one of the bolts and couldn't get down again, and this man "—he indicated his guard—" Joe, you call him, found me on the ledge and brought me along here."

The two seated men looked at one another and spoke together in low tones, which Sam could not hear; then the taller, who seemed to be the leader, rose.

" Lock him in the storeroom, Joe," he ordered. " You can leave the key in the lock. I'll see to him later. Then you'd better get down to the beach and meet that fisherman fellow. You're late now, owing to this young cub's inquisitiveness. He'll be wondering what has become of you."

" Okay, guv'nor," said Joe, taking hold of Jack's arm. " You come along with me," he added, pulling him towards the door as the two men turned away, again conversing in low tones.

Sam had been so interested in the scene before him

that he only just realized his peril in time. He tiptoed down the steps and backed away down the passage as the door opened and Jack and his captor came through, and only the fact that the sudden transition from the lightness of the room to the darkness of the passage robbed them momentarily of sight, saved him from being discovered, for he was in full view and saw them plainly.

The man Joe kept a firm grip on Jack's arm as, with his free hand, he took a key from his pocket and inserted it in the lock. Opening the door, he pushed the boy inside, pulled the door to again and relocked it.

While his attention was thus engaged, Sam worked quickly. He had decided on his plan of action. Once round the first bend in the passage, he slipped off his sea-boots and, holding them in his hands, took to his heels. On reaching the fork, he paused a moment, then turned to the left and ran on another thirty yards or so. Stopping, he switched off his torch and waited.

Presently he heard the sound of approaching foot-steps. When he caught Jack, the man Joe had used the other cave. For the success of Sam's plan it was necessary that he should do so now. If he did not— well, Sam braced his young muscles and waited.

The footfalls drew nearer and, heralded by the beam from his torch, Joe appeared in the opening. After a moment of suspense, he turned to the right, and Sam, peeping round the corner, breathed a sigh of relief.

As soon as Joe was well down the passage, Sam hurriedly retraced his way to the room at the foot of the steps. Joe had done as he had been bidden. The key was in the lock. Without more ado Sam turned it and opened the door.

Jack, his hands deep in his pockets, was sitting on the chest with, it must be confessed, rather a dejected expression on his face, but at the sound of the opening door he sat up and faced round defiantly.

" Hist," whispered Sam. " I'm a friend. It's me, Sam Tonkin. You remember, don't you? Come quickly. Follow me."

Jack started to his feet in astonishment, but instantly grasped the situation, and, wasting no time in useless questioning, followed the young fisherman into the passage, which they had barely reached when the door at the top of the steps opened and the taller of the two men whom Sam had seen seated at the table appeared in the opening, obviously with the intention of paying his promised visit to Jack.

" Run," whispered Sam, after a momentary hesitation. " Run for your life. Down the passage. Quick."

Jack needed no second bidding. He took to his heels with Sam close behind him, but they were too late to escape detection. As luck would have it, the man, unlike Joe, had switched on his torch before opening the door, and its powerful beam pierced the darkness.

" Is that you, Joe?" came his voice in accents of surprise; then the tone changed. " Who's that?" he challenged. " Stop. Stop, or I'll shoot."

Sam and Jack paid no attention to this exhortation, which, to them, savoured of the old invitation, " Dilly,

Dilly, come and be killed," and continued their headlong flight. A moment later there was a flash, and the
roar of an explosion echoed down the passage. To his
dismay, Jack heard Sam give a gasp of pain.

" What is it? Are you hit?" he cried, half stopping.

But a push in the back and a gasping, " On, on,"
made him resume his flight. Forty yards farther on,
Sam called to him to stop. Luckily they had reached
another elbow in the passage, so were out of sight of
their pursuer, and momentarily safe from another shot.

" I'm hit," gasped Sam. " He got me in the leg. I
can't run any more. Here, take these climbing irons
and the torch, and get away."

" But I can't leave you," protested Jack.

" You must," urged Sam. " You must. There's
no other way. He's coming and if he finds us here,
with his gun, he'll have the pair of us. My leg's hurt.
I can't climb. You must fetch the police. Oh, take
them and run, or it will be too late."

" Go on. It's our only chance," the young fisherman
reiterated, forcing the irons into Jack's reluctant hands.
" Run. I'll keep him back if I can."

Jack hated to leave a comrade in distress, but he
realized that there was no alternative. He could do no
good by staying, while by going he might be able to
bring help.

With a hurried, " Good-bye. I'll go straight to the
police," he gripped the irons and ran on down the
passage.

At the fork he hesitated. There were two possible

ways of descent open to him. He had to think quickly. If he took the right arm, returning the way he had come, he might encounter the man Joe, for he appeared to use that way, while, if he tried the other cave, he was facing the unknown, for it was possible that the holes were not bored for the full length of the descent. There was little time left in which to make a choice. For good or ill, he decided to try the unknown.

A few moments later he reached the end of the passage. Here there was no ledge, as in the other cave. The passage simply ended in the sheer drop into the cave itself. Squatting down, he hastily adjusted the irons on his feet, listening intently the while for sounds of pursuit and feeling relief that he had heard no further shot, which would have meant that poor Sam had been finished out of hand.

As he adjusted the loops round his wrists, he heard the dreaded sound of approaching footsteps echoing down the passage. Swinging himself over the edge, he felt for the first hole with his spurred foot. More then once in his hurried descent he nearly lost his hold and fell, for he knew there was no time to spare, and he took chances which he would never have dreamed of taking in cold blood. He was still some ten feet above the floor of the cave when a bright light began to flicker from the opening high above his head. Evidently his pursuer was nearing the end of the passage. With a hasty glance below, he swung himself outward and dropped.

Although he bent his knees, he fell heavily and rolled

over in the soft sand. Shaken, but not otherwise hurt, he scrambled to his feet at once. Unluckily, his teeth had lost their grip on the torch in the shock of the fall, which had also jolted out the light. Hurriedly he fumbled for the torch, for in the darkness he did not know in which direction the exit lay, but his searching fingers encountered nothing but the yielding sand.

The light above grew stronger. With discovery imminent, he gave up the hopeless search and flung himself at the foot of the wall, scooping the loose sand over his tell-tale white shorts and then pressing his body, with face and hands well hidden, close against the rock.

He was only just in time. A moment later the beam of the torch was stabbing the darkness. It was a much more powerful one than his own, and its penetrating ray roamed searchingly over the floor of the cave. For a few seconds it rested directly on him, and Jack, thinking he was discovered, expected to hear the shattering roar of the revolver and feel the shock of the bullet, but he managed to keep his nerve and lie still, and a few moments later was able to draw a breath of relief as the beam moved on. From that height, the man had failed to distinguish him, lying as he did at the junction of sand and rock.

Still the light wandered round the cave and then suddenly disappeared altogether, leaving Jack in pitch darkness. He lay still for a while, fearing a trap and that the beam might suddenly shoot forth again, then he realized that his enemy could not know which passage he had taken in his retreat, and had probably come to this, as being the nearest. Now, fearing his quarry might escape, he was probably hurrying to the other cave.

He slipped off the irons and groped his way across the cave in the direction where, by the light of his enemy's torch, he had seen the exit to lie, but though he had, as he thought, marked the position carefully, he was at fault. When he had crossed the floor of the cave, his outstretched hands encountered solid rock, and there was no glimmer of light.

Feeling his way carefully to the right for some distance, he decided he must be in error and turned back. Groping his way along for what seemed a great distance, he decided to retrace his steps once more. He had only gone a few feet, however, when the futility of this behaviour struck him. He had lost all sense of direction and if he kept on groping, first one way and then the other, he might go on indefinitely. The only safe plan was to circumnavigate the cave in one direction; so once more he turned back, and at long last was rewarded by a glimpse of daylight at the farther end of the long tunnel-like entrance.

A few moments later he reached the threshold of the cave to see a small figure, hazy and indistinct in the fog, but somehow familiar, pursued by a larger one, dash past.

CHAPTER XIV

The Fight on the Beach

Left to himself in the cave, Tony waited anxiously for news of his friend. The time passed slowly, and he had difficulty in controlling his impatience. Sometimes he stood stock still to listen for any sound from the ledge above, sometimes he moved restlessly, fidgeting with his feet in the sand, and every now and again he retreated to the entrance of the cave for a moment, where the light enabled him to note the slow passing of the time.

Half an hour had passed when at long last he saw a glimmer of light above the ledge, and a few moments later the full glare of an electric torch stabbed the darkness.

" Have you found him? Is he there?" he called, unable to restrain his impatience for news.

A low reply which he could not catch came down to him, then Sam—he could see by the size that it was not Jack—swung himself over the ledge and commenced to climb down.

" Where is he? Isn't he there?" Tony called again, and then realized that Sam would have the torch in his teeth, and would be effectually muzzled until he had finished the descent. He waited with what patience he could muster for the young fisherman to reach the ground.

As he climbed lower, a sudden misgiving shot through Tony. Was it Sam after all? A second later, he was sure. This man was too heavily built. Of course, it was the man he and Jack had seen in the cave earlier in the day, the man who had lost the irons.

His brain in a whirl of doubt, Tony hesitated what to do. The man dropped the last few feet to the ground, turned quickly and seized the boy by the arm.

" Got you!" The exclamation was a whisper, almost to himself. Then he shone his torch in Tony's face. " Who is it you're wanting, anyway?"

" My friend," said Tony, standing passive in the man's grasp. "He climbed up and lost the climbing irons that we found. I went to get another bar to help him."

" Oh, so there were two of you?"

Tony felt the man's eyes searching his face in the darkness. " Does anyone else know he's up there?"

For a moment Tony was going to mention Sam, then something counselled caution. He shook his head, wondering at the same time what had become of the young fisherman.

" Wait a minute. I'll take you to see your friend."

He loosed the boy's arm and stooped to unbuckle the climbing irons from his feet. Although he no longer held Tony, he had, either by accident or design, hemmed him in between a projection of rock and the wall of the cave, and barred the way to the entrance with his body.

Tony thought quickly. There was funny work, as Sam had called it, afoot. Of that there was no doubt. Not for a moment did he trust the man, nor did he believe he meant to take him to see Jack. He had seized him roughly, and Tony had not missed the tone of his muttered " Got you!" The man had removed one iron and was stooping to undo the second. It was now or never.

Drawing as far back as possible to gain all the distance he could, Tony braced his muscles and launched himself with all his weight in a football charge at his captor. Taken completely unawares by this sudden onslaught, the man, emitting a startled oath, rolled over on his back.

Instantly Tony leaped over his prostrate form and made a dash for the exit. As he did so, the man Joe, for it was he, flung the climbing iron. As ill luck would have it, the strap encircled one ankle while Tony's other foot trod on the iron itself, and he crashed to the ground in his turn.

It took him a moment to free his ankle from the strap, and he scrambled to his feet to find his opponent close upon him, but he dashed out of the cave with a two-yard lead.

Tony was fleet of foot and was, in fact, the fastest sprinter in his form, but his fall had " winded " him slightly, so he could not run his fastest, and to his dismay he found his pursuer was gaining on him, and could sense the outstretched hand reaching for his collar.

Desperate situations require desperate remedies.

On the verge of capture, he recalled the old, old trick so often played when " ragging " with his friends at school, and instantly decided to make use of it. Stopping dead in his tracks, he stooped low. The ruse succeeded. Totally unsuspecting and unprepared for the trap, the man tripped over him and sprawled on his face in the sand, while Tony was rolled over by the collision.

Both scrambled to their feet at once, but Tony, not being taken by surprise, was the quicker of the two, and gained a few yards' start. Along the beach he fled, with his enemy pounding in hot pursuit. In spite of his bulk, Joe could run and, strive as he would, Tony could not shake him off.

The soft sand made the going heavy, and Tony found himself panting, while he could hear the heavy breathing of his enemy close behind him. In this fashion, a few yards apart, they passed the entrance to the first cave, out of which Jack emerged just in time to see them race by.

A moment sufficed for Jack to take in the situation. That neither pursuer nor pursued had seen him was obvious, so, unknown to both, he joined in the race and pounded along a bad third.

Still holding his few yards' lead, Tony reached the foot of the cliff path and started to bound up it like a mountain goat. Scattered along the edge of the sand, at the cliff foot, lay a smattering of loose stones. Joe stooped quickly, picked up a large round stone and, as Jack, who saw the vile deed, gasped with horror, hurled it at the flying Tony.

At such short range it was almost impossible to miss.

It struck the boy in the small of the back—the spot of the vicious "kidney punch" of the old-time American boxer—and with a dreadful groaning cry Tony fell forward. In a dozen strides, the man was on him and, half kneeling, half squatting across his prostrate form, he held his sides and threw back his head as he breathed in great gasps, struggling to regain his breath.

Jack stopped dead. He was directly behind Joe, who had no idea of his presence. His first horror at the dastardly attack—for stone throwing to a true British boy savours of hitting "below the belt"—gave way to a wave of hot anger as a moment later he saw Tony writhe helplessly and utter a moan of pain.

Seething with rage, Jack realized that it was no time for squeamishness. If his chum was to be rescued, he must fight the enemy with the weapons of his own choosing. Swiftly his eye selected a suitable shingle of some three or four pounds' weight. He picked it up and, cautiously stepping nearer to his unconscious victim, took careful aim and let fly.

His aim was good. The stone caught the man behind his right ear, and without even a groan he collapsed on top of Tony.

Snatching up a second stone, Jack leaped forward with it poised ready, if necessary, to give the *coup de grâce*, but there was no need. Joe was knocked out, and lay completely unconscious.

It required no little effort to roll him off Tony, who could do little to help himself, but Jack managed it, and was not unduly tender in the process. Then he helped his chum to his feet.

Tony's face was twisted with pain, but he managed to smile wanly when he recognized Jack.

" You've escaped, then. Jolly good," he murmured in a weak voice.

" Yes, thanks to Sam," said Jack. " But come on, we've no time to lose. Sam is still up there in the passage. They shot him in the leg, and the fellow who did it is after me, and may be along any minute."

" Had I better hit that fellow again?" he suggested, with a look of hatred at the prostrate Joe. " I'd tie him up, but I doubt if there's time."

But to strike a man when he was down—even such an unscrupulous enemy as Joe had shown himself to be—was more than Jack could bring himself to do; so, leaving him still lying unconscious—indeed he had not even moved since his first collapse—the boys started up the steep slope.

Tony's back was very painful, and their progress was slow, so that long before they reached the top Jack had a supporting arm round his friend, and was casting anxious glances behind him, fearing to see a man's form loom out of the fog in pursuit of them, but at length they gained the summit unmolested.

" Now where do we go?" asked Jack.

" I've been wondering which will be the quickest," said Tony. " Into the village, or to the Watch House. There's a telephone at the Watch House. We'd better go there, I think."

Tony's back was growing easier and, though he still pressed a hand to his side, he could dispense with Jack's arm, and they were able to make better speed along the comparatively level path, but Jack, still fearful of pursuit, did not breathe freely until the little hut loomed out of the mist ahead.

To their delight, they found Tom Wallis on duty, and he listened in open-mouthed astonishment as they, somewhat disjointedly, gave him an outline of their adventure.

" Well," he said, " if this don't beat all. You say they shot young Sam, and he's still up there in the passage. This is a job for the police all right, or maybe I'd better ring up the Major, but you say he's away?"

" He was, but he may be back by now," said Tony.

Tom Wallis rang up the Hall to find that Major Bamford had that moment returned. After the first few sentences of explanation, Tom laid the receiver down.

" Your father said he's coming straight up here. You're to wait for him."

A few minutes later, the boys, standing in the door-way, saw Major Bamford breasting the slope at the double, followed by Simpson, the village constable, whom he had picked up en route, the chauffeur and old David Ellis, the gardener.

" Now," he said, entering the hut and seating himself at the table. " What is this astonishing story? Tell me."

CHAPTER XV

The Empty House

" This is serious," said the Major, when he had heard the boys' story. " Three men you say there were, Jack? There may, of course, be others whom you did not see. They have arms too, and do not hesitate to make use of them."

He shook his head thoughtfully.

" This is too big a job for us to tackle alone, Simpson," he went on.

Simpson, the constable, his genial face unduly solemn for once, nodded agreement.

" We'd better telephone to Dovermouth for help, sir," he suggested.

" I will, and at once," said the Major. " But meanwhile you had better take Ellis and Johnson and see if you can lay your hands on the man Joe."

" Very good, sir," agreed Simpson readily. " Come along, you two."

As the men turned to leave, Tom Wallis unlocked a cupboard door.

" Here," he said, producing a couple of stout sticks

159

with crooked handles. " Take these along. They'll maybe come in useful."

" Thank ye," said old David Ellis, with a knowing nod. " Maybe they will."

" They're sword sticks," whispered Tony to Jack.

" Don't force things," counselled Major Bamford as the men left the hut. " If the fellow hasn't recovered from Tony's knock-out blow, bring him along, but be careful. He may be armed. If he has gone, you'd better watch the beach, and one of you come back to report to me."

Turning, he picked up the telephone.

" Dovermouth, one two five two, sir," said Tom Wallis, who had quietly looked out the number.

" Good work. Thanks very much," commented the Major.

A few moments later he was speaking to the sergeant in charge of the police station at Dovermouth. Listening to one end of a telephone conversation is never very satisfactory, and can be exceedingly annoying, but it was soon obvious to the boys watching Major Bamford's expression and hearing his remarks that all was not as he would have wished.

" That's awkward, very awkward," he said, as he replaced the receiver. " It seems that a prisoner has escaped from the gaol, and all the available police are out forming a cordon round the area where it is thought the man is hiding. The sergeant has promised to get in touch with the inspector and to send some men along as soon as he can, but, scattered as they are, there is bound to be some delay. However, this is far more important than an escaped prisoner, and I have no doubt but that they will do their best.

"Now," he went on, "the question is, can we identify the house to which the passage from the cave leads? You say you think it was several hundred yards in length, Jack?"

"Yes, sir," said Jack. "A good quarter of a mile at the very least."

"There are only two houses possible, I should say, sir," put in Tom Wallis. "There's the Homestead. That's got new people in it. They've only been there a few weeks."

"Yes," agreed the Major. "A Mr. and Mrs. Constantine, I believe, but I have not met them yet."

"Nobody in the village knows much about them, sir," went on Tom. "They brought their own servants with them, and buy very little in the village shops. Most of their stuff comes down from London, so they say."

"And the other house you suspect will be Sandersfoot, I suppose," said the Major. "Sandersfoot is empty, is it not?"

"It is, sir," said Wallis. "But someone might be using it and nobody know they are there. There's no caretaker."

"Um," grunted Major Bamford thoughtfully. "They're both old houses, so both are possible. We'll go to see the vicar," he announced, standing up. "He may have met the Constantines and may know something about them. Ring me up at the vicarage if there is any news, Wallis."

"Ay, ay, sir," answered Wallis, using the age-old reply of the seaman.

"Come, boys."

A few minutes later saw Major Bamford and our two friends ringing the vicarage bell, and soon they were closeted with the vicar in his study.

"Good gracious me, Major," cried that startled man when he had heard the news. "I can hardly believe my ears. Such disgraceful actions, and in our quiet little village too of all places. No," he went on after a pause. "I don't know the Constantines at all, so I fear I cannot help you much. I called, of course, but the servant said that they were out. They never come to church, and I've never actually set eyes on them. But you say young Tonkin is wounded? Something must be done, Major; something must be done."

"I've sent for the police, as I told you," replied the Major a little testily. "Ah, is that the telephone?"

The vicar picked up the receiver on his desk.

"It's for you, Major," he said, handing it over a moment later. "Tom Wallis wants to speak to you."

Tom Wallis's report was the cheering news that a police sergeant and a dozen constables were on their way by car and would arrive in a little under an hour; also, that Ellis had returned to the hut to say that there was no sign of the man Joe on the beach, where Simpson and Johnson had remained to keep watch.

" Right," said the Major. " Let Ellis rejoin them and report anything that occurs at once."

" Major," said the vicar, " I hate this inaction. Suppose I go and call again on the Constantines. I might be able to learn something."

" Do so by all means," agreed Major Bamford. " You two boys could make yourselves useful too," he continued. " Go to Sandersfoot and see if there is a sign of anything stirring there. But remember," he warned, " don't be too venturesome, and if you see anything at all suspicious, come straight back and report to me here. We'll make this our headquarters, if you have no objection, vicar. It is so much more central and nearer the scene of action than the Hall."

Nothing loth, Tony and Jack set off through the fog once more at a steady trot, and soon entered the lane leading to Sandersfoot. The house stood in its own grounds of several acres, which were surrounded by a high lichen-covered brick wall, pierced at one point by high wooden gates from which the green paint was peeling off. Tony tried the iron handle, but the gate refused to move.

" Give me a leg up," he said.

Jack hoisted him up and held him while he peered over the top of the gates.

" There's a long gravel drive—it doesn't look as if it had been weeded for months—and big banks of rhododendrons on each side," he reported.

" Can you see the house?"

" No. The drive winds away to the right. I might be able to see the house if it wasn't for the fog."

" How is the gate fastened?" puffed Jack, who found Tony growing heavy. " Is it locked?"

" I don't think so. Just a wooden bar."

" Climb over then and open it."

Jack gave a final hoist and Tony, with a scramble, got a leg over the gate. He sat astride for a moment, looking about, and then dropped to the ground on the inside. Jack heard the sound of a bar being pulled back and the gate opened to admit him.

" We'll just push the gate to and leave it unbarred," said Tony, suiting his action to his words.

Together they cautiously advanced up the drive, walking on the grass border so that their footsteps should make no sound on the protruding stones of the gravel. As they rounded the bend at the end of the shrubbery, the house came in sight. It was a grim looking stone building, topped by tall chimneys and almost surrounded by high trees. The lower windows were shuttered, and the place had a neglected air as though long shut up.

From the shelter of a bush the boys reconnoitred for a time, taking in the details and making sure that the coast was clear, then they warily worked their way round to the back, which looked as desolate and deserted as the front had done. Growing bolder, they followed a path which led round the farther side of the house. As they reached a corner, Jack, who happened to be in the lead, gave a gasp of surprise

and leaped backwards, colliding with Tony so that the
two of them rolled over on the ground.

" What's up?" demanded the startled Tony in a
whisper.

" There's a man there. Look out! He may be
coming this way."

Scrambling to their feet, the boys stood listening.
Distant footsteps sounded on the gravel. They drew
nearer, then, as the boys prepared to run, stopped.

Gaining courage, Tony peeped round the corner.
A man stood in the little porch of a side door and, as
Tony watched, he lifted the knocker and knocked in a
peculiar manner—three quick raps, then two more at
intervals.

After a pause the door was opened and a man's
voice greeted the visitor.

" It's you at last, is it?" said the voice grumpily.
" Where have you been all this time? I thought you
were never coming."

" The motor let me down," said the man at the door.
" I had to——" But his explanation was cut short.

" Oh, come in, come in," cried the voice. The man
disappeared inside and the door was shut.

The boys looked at one another.

" Run back and tell Dad," whispered Tony. " I'll
wait here."

" How did the fellow get in?" whispered Jack in
return. " He can't have come up the drive. He
wouldn't know the gate was loose. There must be
another entrance. Let's find out."

Keeping a wary eye on the door, they approached to find a path leading away at right angles to the house. Following it, they came to a small door in the outer wall which opened on to the down itself. An old Ford van, such as shopkeepers use for delivering goods, stood outside.

" I'll stay and watch here," said Tony. " You get along and tell Dad."

" All right," agreed Jack. " But keep out of sight. Don't let the fellow catch you."

Breaking into a trot, he was soon lost in the fog.

Tony looked round. A nearby furze bush offered excellent cover and, taking refuge behind it, he settled himself to wait and watch. The minutes ticked away slowly with no sign from the silent house, and at length he began to tire of the monotony. The fog seemed worse too, and, possibly because of his in-action, the damp of it seemed to strike through his clothes and he felt chilly. He decided to take a peep at the house.

Leaving his hiding-place, he approached the door in the wall. He had grasped the handle, and his thumb had lifted the latch when he heard a move-ment on the farther side. Shuffling footsteps were approaching. In a momentary panic he dropped the latch, which fell with an audible click, and turned to flee.

" Who's there?" came in challenging tones.

He had barely time to dodge behind the van when the door was wrenched open and a man leapt out, looking up and down.

" There's no one here, Bill," he said.

" Are you sure?" replied Bill, stepping out in his turn.

" Look for yourself. You're as jumpy as a cat," said the first man in a disgusted voice.

Hidden by the van, Tony stood still, his heart pounding in his ribs. Longingly he looked at his friendly furze bush, but it was a good thirty feet away, and to reach it he must cross the open in full view of the men. Bitterly he blamed himself for his impatience, which had led him to leave its friendly shelter, but it was too late now. By stooping he could see the men's feet under the van.

" Are you sure, Tom?" repeated Bill. " I'll swear I heard something."

Less easily satisfied than his mate, he started to walk round the van. Tony saw his feet at the rear. For a moment he hesitated, weighing the chances of a quick dash over the heath. Forty yards' start and he would be lost in the fog, but there were two men and they might run him down. The man Tom looked young and might be fleet of foot. His hesitation settled the question. He realized that it was too late for flight. Silently he slipped between the wheels and crouched on the turf under the van itself.

Bill walked right round the van, peering into the fog, before he was satisfied.

" I could ha' sworn I heard something," he said again.

" Maybe you did," said Tom, with a hoarse laugh.
" Maybe a squirrel knocked a nut off a tree and it
dropped on the wall."

" That's so," said Bill doubtfully, not quite sure
whether his mate was serious or merely trying to pull
his leg.

" Come on," said Tom impatiently. " We can't
stand here all day. Let's get the stuff aboard."

Together they carried out a packing case, which,
by their grunts and ejaculations, was evidently weighty,
and lifted it into the van. Bill climbed in, his heavy
boots crushing the boards just over Tony's head as
he stowed the case to his satisfaction. He jumped
down at last and, with Tom, disappeared through the
garden door.

Once sure that the door was closed, Tony wasted
no time in scrambling out from under the van, and
again took refuge behind the furze bush. From this
hiding-place he watched the men carry out two more
packing cases and load them into the van. Then,
having shut the garden door, Bill climbed up into
the driver's seat and pressed the starter. Tom
scrambled up beside his mate and the van rolled
away, to be lost, a few moments later, in the shrouding
fog.

" Phew!" whistled Tony, as he stood up. " I wonder
what they are up to."

There being nothing more to see, he walked round
the wall to the big entrance gates and on down the
lane up which he knew his father would come. He

had only proceeded a few yards when he heard the tramp of approaching feet, and a moment later he recognized his father's voice. It was Major Bamford with Jack and the promised dozen stalwart policemen in charge of a sergeant.

" Is that you, Tony?" hailed his father, as they caught sight of each other through the fog. " Well, what has happened? I thought Jack left you watching the side gate."

In as few words as possible, Tony told his news.

" Gone, have they? You are sure they did not take young Tonkin with them?"

" Quite, Dad. There were only the two of them."

" The cases were not big enough to hold him, were they?" suggested Jack.

" No," said Tony, with a slight shudder at the idea of his friend's body being hidden in a packing case. " Not unless they cut him up," he added.

" That's not likely, thank goodness," said Major Bamford. " Come, sergeant. We had better search the house and find the passage to the cave."

Entering by the big gates, the party advanced up the drive and made for the side door which the men had used. The sergeant turned the handle, then set his shoulder to the door and pushed, but it resisted his efforts.

" Locked," he commented.

" Shall we burst it in, or find another way?" asked the Major.

" Look here," cried Tony, who had stepped into

what had once been a flower bed. " This soil is all trampled and see, this shutter is loose."

The shutter was on a small window above the bed, and it swung back on its hinges at his touch.

" Ah!" said the sergeant as he stepped across to investigate. " You'd make a good detective, young sir. Here's where they got in, sir, obviously," he went on, turning to the Major. " The shutter has been forced and the catch of the window pushed back with a knife. It's loose.

" Once inside, they'd use the side door and, when they left, they dropped the latch again. Now, who'll climb through and open the door?" he went on, turning to his subordinates. " This window is none too big. James, you're the smallest. See if you can manage it."

Constable James, helped by two of his comrades, gallantly made the attempt, but policemen are usually built on what an outfitter calls " outsize " lines, and strive as he would he could not force his shoulders through the aperture.

" Wait till I get my tunic off," he said at last, with-drawing his head and starting to undo the buttons. But even without his coat his shoulders were still too wide to be manœuvred through the opening.

The boys had been laughing unrestrainedly at his struggles, and even the Major and his brother con-stables had broad grins on their faces.

" Let me try," said Jack, suddenly becoming serious.

" Do you mind, sir?" asked the sergeant. " He'd

get through easily enough, and could open the door for us. We are wasting time that may be precious."

Major Bamford hesitated.

"I don't suppose they have left anyone inside to hurt the boy, but I hesitate to let a guest go. What about you, Tony?"

"I'll go, Dad," said Tony eagerly.

Jack's face fell.

"Let's both go, sir," he suggested. "If there are two of us, we'll take more hurting if there is anyone to attack us."

"We'll burst the door in fast enough if there's any hanky-panky," said the burly sergeant.

"Very well," agreed the Major.

So Tony and Jack were lifted through the window, and found themselves in what was evidently the butler's pantry.

CHAPTER XVI

Sam Disappears

From the pantry the boys peeped cautiously out into the passage. Through a half-open door on the farther side they could see into a big stone-floored kitchen. They listened, but all was quiet in the house. No sound broke the stillness.

Tony stepped out into the passage and tiptoed along in the direction of the side door, Jack following some six feet behind him, keeping a careful watch and ready to give the alarm if he were attacked, but, though they felt distinctly " creepy ", nothing untoward happened, and a moment later Tony had slipped back the catch, the door was open, and the police thronged into the house. Quickly they passed from room to room.

" Now, young gentlemen," said the sergeant, turning to the boys, " which of the rooms was it that you saw? Can you tell?"

" I'm not sure," said Tony. " There was a table in it, I know, and these rooms are all empty."

" Can you remember, Jack?" asked Major Bamford. " You were inside some time."

" I know I was," said Jack, grinning a trifle sheepishly. " There was a table and there must have been some chairs, but I didn't notice much. I was watching the men's faces, and was too scared to take stock of what there was."

" Quite," said the Major sympathetically. " I'm not surprised. It was a very unpleasant experience."

" There is nothing in any of the rooms now, sir," said a constable. " They're all empty."

" Yes, but they may have taken the stuff away with them," said the sergeant. " Try to remember, young gentlemen. Was it this room?" he added, leading the way into a long room which was oak panelled to a height of six feet or so all round the walls.

" I can't say for certain," said Jack, looking round him with rather a puzzled expression on his face. " But I'm sure of one thing. If this is not the room, none of the others is."

" Good enough!" cried the sergeant. " Come on, men, try the walls."

Systematically he and his men commenced to examine the panelling, tapping it at intervals, seeking for the hollow sound which would betray the entrance to the passage, but though they had one or two false clues, after twenty minutes' careful work they had to own themselves beaten.

" We must try the cave, sir," said the sergeant. " There's nothing else for it. I'll leave three of my men here to keep guard, and the rest of us had better go to the cave."

As they left the house they met the vicar.

"I was looking for you, Major," he said, falling into step alongside Major Bamford. "I called on the Constantines. The door was open and Mr. Constantine was in the hall, so I saw him. He's a charming fellow, though I must say his nerves are in a terrible state. When a door slammed at the back of the house somewhere, he jumped to his feet and stood listening. Then he apologized and said that his nerves are all to pieces. It seems he was shell-shocked in the war and has never been fit since. That is why he lives such a quiet, retired life and sees practically no one but his wife and servants. He's an awfully nice fellow, though, and has asked me to call again."

"Um," said the Major. "That rules out the Homestead, but I think we're on the right track here. We're just off to the caves. We must find young Tonkin at all costs."

Tramping over the down through the fog, they soon reached the cliff path to the beach and descended in single file. At the entrance to the first cave they found Johnson and Ellis mounting guard.

"Nothing to report, sir," said Ellis cheerfully. "Not a sight nor sound of anything inside, and I believe it's the same farther up, for Simpson said he would hail us if he heard anything."

"Good," said the Major, and leaving the two men, reinforced by a couple of constables, at their posts, the party continued their way along the beach.

As they neared the second cave, they expected to be

challenged, and to see Simpson waiting for them, but no challenge came.

" Hullo! Simpson! Where are you?" hailed Major Bamford.

There was no reply.

" That's funny," commented the Major. " Where's Simpson got to? I wonder what can have become of him."

He shouted again, with like result.

" Look there, sir, what's that?" cried Jack, whose quick eyes had caught sight of a dark, shapeless bundle lying on the sands close to the rocks at the side of the cave.

A few strides and the sergeant was bending over it.

" Is this the missing man, sir?" he said, turning to the Major.

It was. The unfortunate Simpson lay bound hand and foot, with a handkerchief stuffed into his mouth and tied in place with another one.

" There's been rough play here," said the sergeant, who, having removed the handkerchief, held it up to show that, where it had passed round the back of the neck, it was soaked with blood. " He's been hit good and proper. He's unconscious by the look of him."

The gag was removed and still Simpson lay inert, but, as his bonds were cut, he opened his eyes and looked wonderingly round at the ring of faces bending over him.

" How are you, Simpson?" asked the Major

solicitously. " You've had a nasty blow. Can you tell us how you came by it?"

Helped by a comrade, Simpson sat up and felt his injured head carefully.

" I can't rightly say, sir. I was standing here watching the caves when I heard a noise behind me, between me and the sea, that is. I turned round to look and—well, I don't remember any more till I woke up here just now."

" I wonder who managed to get behind you?" queried the Major.

" Maybe no one, sir," said the sergeant. " It's dark in the mouth of the cave and a man could stand in there and see out when you couldn't see in. Maybe they tossed a stone past him when he glanced away. He heard it fall and it caught his attention, then, when he turned round to look, they took the chance to rush him. It's an old enough trick. I've worked it myself. It came in mighty useful once when I had an armed man to deal with. Now we'd better search the caves."

Major Bamford wished to leave Simpson in charge of the boys, but he professed himself better and got manfully to his feet, though it was obvious that he was still more than a trifle shaky.

Both the caves were searched at once, but were untenanted.

" Is there any way up from this beach other than the path we came down by?" asked the sergeant.

" None," said the Major.

" Then they could not have got away without being

seen by your men," said the sergeant. " They must
have gone back to the passage."

" Unless they went away by sea, Dad," put in Tony.
" Sam came in his boat, I expect, and she would still
be there."

" We've seen no sign of her," said his father, glancing
seaward. " But with this fog, if she were moored a
little way out, we might not be able to see her."

" We'll leave that for the present," said the sergeant,
who felt more at home on terra firma and had no
wish to go afloat. " Now what about that patent step-
ladder of yours, young gentlemen?"

The boys showed the sergeant where the holes in
the rock were situated. As they left the house, a man
had been dispatched to the village to bring all the bolts
of the size that Tony had bought that the shop had in
stock and a long rope, and he had arrived with a good-
sized bag full of them.

" Now," said the sergeant, " who'll volunteer to
lead the climb?"

" I will, sir," came from all the constables in chorus.
The sergeant smiled.

" Good lads. Well, Smithson, you have the bag of
bolts. Suppose you try."

Slinging the bag round his neck and looping the
end of the rope over his shoulder, the policeman began
to climb, but as he placed a bolt in each hole he left
it in place, so that as he climbed he left a series of
bolts projecting from the face of the rock. Higher and
higher he climbed, his comrades below paying out the

rope so that it ran clear and did not impede his movements. They also shone their powerful torches aloft so that the opening of the passage was clearly visible.

"I don't like this, sergeant," said Major Bamford, shaking his head as the policeman reached the half-way line. "One man up there with a revolver could hold up the lot of us."

"That's true enough, sir, but we've got to try it," said the sergeant with a shrug. "There's no sign of them yet, and you must remember that smuggling is one thing, but murder is another, and while a man may be ready enough at the first, he'll hesitate at the second."

"I hope so," said the Major, "though one of them did not hesitate to shoot young Tonkin."

"That's true, sir," agreed the sergeant; "but still—duty is duty."

All eyes watched the climbing man with an anxiety that grew as he rose higher above them and neared the forbidding circle of darkness. His progress was necessarily slow, for with each step upwards he had to extricate a bolt from the bag suspended round his neck and fix it in place. At long last he reached his goal and drew himself into the opening. For a few moments he disappeared, but his light could be seen glowing in the tunnel. The rope jerked, then his face appeared over the edge.

"All fast!" he called cheerily. "There is no one in sight up here."

A second policeman at once commenced to climb. Pulling himself up hand over hand and using the bolts for footholds, he was soon at the top, and no sooner was he clear of the rope than another followed. Major Bamford followed the sergeant at the end of the procession.

" What about us?" whispered Jack, nudging Tony, as the Major mounted the rock face.

" Shut up. We'll follow on, but, if we ask, he may order us not to."

As soon as the Major had disappeared, the boys followed. The passage seemed full of men and the glare from the torches lit up the rocky walls. The leading police had already explored the passage to the farther cave and shouted to their comrades below, who were standing by to see that the quarry did not escape by one bolt-hole as the pursuers entered by the other. The sergeant now prepared to explore the main passage.

" I'd forgotten you two," said the Major, catching sight of the boys. " I might have known you'd follow, but I never gave it a thought. However, as you are here, you may stay and see it through. I fancy we're too late and the birds have flown."

With the sergeant in the lead and the boys unwillingly bringing up the rear, the party marched in single file up the zig-zag passage. They traversed it without incident, save that the sergeant noticed a few drops of blood at a spot where, doubtless, young Tonkin had stood when wounded, but there was no sign of him and they reached the little room at the foot of the flight of steps without encountering anyone.

The door of the room was ajar. The sergeant pushed it open and entered. It was empty, as was also the big chest, which stood with its huge lid gaping wide.

Turning, the sergeant mounted the stairs and put his eye to the spy hole.

" No one in sight," he announced, and, quickly mastering the mechanism of the door, swung it open.

" Hullo!" he shouted, stepping through. " Wright, Jackson, Thomas, where are you?"

There was no response.

" This is not the room," said the Major, who had followed him in. " It's very similar. The window and the fireplace are in the same places, but the panelling goes right up to the ceiling."

" So it does," said the sergeant.

" It's a different house altogether, sir," said one of the constables, who had crossed to the door and opened it. " The hall is different."

" So it is!" cried the sergeant again, striding into the hall and opening a door on the farther side. " Why, this room is furnished. Which house can it be? Is anyone here?"

A quick search revealed that the house was tenantless, but it was obvious that it had only recently been vacated and that the late tenants had wasted little time in packing. Only a few of the rooms were furnished and

in these confusion reigned. Drawers had been dragged
out and their contents tossed out on the floor as the
owner had searched for a particular article.

" Surely," said the Major suddenly, " this must be
the Homestead."

Opening the front door, he stepped out into the drive
and looked up at the house.

" Yes," he said, " it is. So we've been barking up
the wrong tree, sergeant. It isn't Sandersfoot after all,
though there is evidently something fishy going on
there too. No wonder Mr. Constantine was rather
nervous. I wonder what the vicar will have to say
about the charming fellow when he hears."

" Where's the garage?" asked the sergeant suddenly.

" Round at this side, if I remember rightly," said
Major Bamford, leading the way.

The garage doors were gaping wide and it was empty,
but fresh tracks in the damp gravel showed that two
cars had recently been driven away.

" Too late, sergeant," commented the Major.

" Looks like it, sir, but we may lay our hands on
them yet," said that worthy. " I wonder what those two
birds were up to at the other house. No good, I'll
warrant."

" Where will we be going next?" asked Tony of his
father a few minutes later. They were back in the
house, where the police were executing a thorough
search for anything which might give them a clue
and put them on the trail.

" Home," said the Major, with a meaning smile.

"You two have had quite a big enough day. Off you go now. I'll come along as soon as I can, but supper and bed for you, and at once."

"Pity you spoke," said Jack, laughing, as they took their way down the winding lane in the direction of the Hall.

CHAPTER XVII

The Steam Yacht "Medusa"

Major Bamford did not return until late that evening, and it was not until the next morning at breakfast that the boys saw him again.

Naturally the adventures of the day before were the topic of conversation to the exclusion of all else.

The Major told the boys what had happened after he had sent them home. The Constantines had got clear away and, in spite of a description of the cars, which were known in the village, being telephoned to the police in the surrounding districts, no one could say definitely that he had seen them, though a vague report had come in that a car which might or might not be one of them had passed through the village of Monksraston, about ten miles away. After that all trace had been lost.

" What about the other house, sir? Had the two men there anything to do with it?" asked Jack.

The Major laughed.

" That really is rather amusing. It completely deceived us. As a matter of fact, they were acting quite independently and had nothing to do with these

miscreants at all. They had taken advantage of the
house being shut up and empty to rifle it of all the
lead piping and sheeting that they could cut off, and
they made a very thorough job of it. When they had
it all nicely packed, one of the men went for the van
to carry it away, and you came on the scene just in
the nick of time and saw him.

"The police roped them in absolutely red-handed.
When we sent out a description of the Constantines'
cars, we gave one of the van as well, and it was stopped
by a police patrol just outside Dovermouth, with its
load of lead still aboard."

"What a sell for them!" commented Jack.

"Is there no news of Sam Tonkin?" asked Tony.

"None," said the Major, shaking his head. "None
at all. He's vanished with the rest of them. It's very
puzzling and very distressing. His grandparents are
terribly worried and upset."

"What's it all about, Dad?" asked Tony. "What
have they been doing? We don't understand it a bit,
do we, Jack?"

Jack shook his head in agreement.

"You've heard of the 'dope' traffic?" went on the
Major after a pause. "How cocaine, and other drugs—
excellent in the hands of the medical profession, but
dangerous when their use is abused—are being brought
into the country and sold at enormous profit.

"It is, of course, against the law to deal in the
stuff, except through the proper channels, so these
people smuggle it in. Smuggling was bad enough in

the old days, but the goods smuggled—mainly spirits and silks—did no great harm in themselves. This dope smuggling comes in a very different category, and does far more harm than merely defrauding the revenue. The vile stuff, in unscrupulous hands, does untold damage. Thoughtless people try it, possibly in fun and as a new experience. It makes them feel cheerful and jolly, so, if they are weak, they try it again to repeat the sensation, and so the habit grows. In other cases people start through illness, when they may take it to deaden pain, but however they begin, should they make a habit of it, it becomes a necessity; the craving for it becomes worse and worse and they need larger doses. In the long run they become slaves to it—physical and mental wrecks—and only feel well when under its influence.

" It has been suspected for some time now that large quantities have been smuggled ashore in this district. You see, it is not bulky, and it is quite easy for a fisherman to bring quite a valuable consignment ashore in his boat."

" Is that what Sam has been doing?" asked Tony.

" I'm afraid so. He probably did not realize the serious thing he was doing, and the evil consequences which might follow."

" I'm sure he didn't," said Tony stoutly in defence of his friend. " He told me it was the new taxes, and that it was only what the old free traders did, and harming nobody but the Government."

The Major shook his head sadly.

"Poor Sam has been getting impatient, I know. The fishing has been a failure, and he has chafed at working so hard and earning so little. Easy money. It is the will o' the wisp that has lured many a man from the right path."

"Poor Sam!" echoed Tony. "I wonder where he is now."

"There was no sign of him, so we may hope for the best, though I believe the men he has to deal with would stick at nothing. Poor old Anne! She broke down completely when I told her the news. She has suspected something for some time, I fancy, but for the boy's sake would say nothing. Old Sam knew more than she did. I'm afraid it will be a long time before he hears the last of it. Anne does not forgive easily and, now it is too late to do any good, she blames him."

The telephone bell rang and a few moments later a maid entered.

"You are wanted on the phone, sir," she said.

The Major was not long before he returned, with a puzzled look on his face.

"Here's news, boys," he said. "Sam's boat has been found by another fisherman, lying at anchor, quite unhurt, about three miles out at sea, close to the fishing ground."

"Was Sam in her?" queried Tony eagerly.

"No. No one aboard, but she is quite undamaged. The fisherman towed her into the cove. She's down there now."

Tony started up.

" Let's go down and have a look at her."

.   .   .   .

It was four days later. The fog had gone at last, to be succeeded by a south-easterly gale, which had kept the boys ashore. Sam's disappearance was still a mystery. There was no news of him. He and his captors seemed to have disappeared into thin air. The police had thoroughly explored the Homestead, sounding the old walls, and had come across a hidey hole over the big fireplace in the panelled room. It was only a small chamber, barely seven feet long by five in width, and had a tiny slit of a window carefully concealed in the stonework of the outside of the house, so that from the ground it was quite invisible. It had evidently been a priest's hiding-place or a refuge for fugitives in days gone by, but there was no sign of recent habitation. The Constantines had been thorough in covering their traces, and nothing had been left to give a clue to their identity or where-abouts. The sergeant and the detectives who followed him confessed themselves baffled.

The weather having settled down again, Tony and Jack—with Mr. Pascoe's permission this time, for, after being blown away, Major Bamford had decreed that they must consult the boatbuilder and get his permission before deciding on their programme for the day afloat—had again put to sea, bound for the fishing grounds.

They were without bait for bottom fishing, so were

dependent on catching some in the form of a mackerel or two before they could anchor.

Under easy canvas, for a boat does not want to go too fast through the water when " mackerelling ", and with a line, ending in a bright spinner, trailing over each quarter, the *Spray* ran leisurely off before the wind to the fishing ground.

Mackerel were scarce and the boys sailed about, first in one direction, then in another, sometimes with a short line and a light weight, or " sinker ", to keep the hook near the top, and sometimes with a heavier lead and a longer line to try in deeper water in case the fish were swimming at a greater depth, but it was useless.

" There doesn't seem to be a mackerel left," said Jack at last in disgust.

He left his line made fast to the rail and stood up by the mast. They were a good three miles off the land and in the fine weather the distant coast was clearly visible.

" I say," he said suddenly, " I believe there's a steam yacht at anchor in Dovermouth Bay."

" So there is," agreed Tony, after standing up in his turn. " It's funny how difficult it is to pick her out against the land and houses beyond, and then, when you do see her, she stands out quite plainly. She looks a big craft."

" I should love to see her close," said Jack.

" Come on, then. Shake out the reefs and set the mizzen. There's no chance of fishing."

" Ought we to go?" asked Jack doubtfully. " We didn't tell old Pascoe we were going to Dovermouth."

" That was because we wanted to go fishing. He'd have let us go to Dovermouth if we'd asked. Don't you remember he said: ' Fine weather and an offshore wind, young gentlemen. You may take your choice to-day. Just say where you want to go and I'll agree ' ?"

" So he did," said Jack, relieved. Major Bamford was " such a good sport " that he felt he would have hated to deceive him.

" Dad wouldn't mind a bit," said Tony. " It isn't as if it was bad weather. It's sure to keep fine."

So the reefs which had been put in, in order to go slow enough to catch the mackerel, were " shaken out ", the mizzen was set and the *Spray* woke up. She was no longer like a lazy little girl, dawdling along almost too sleepy to move, but was full of life, lying over to the stronger puffs, thrusting the little wavelets scornfully aside with her bold bow and leaving a white wake behind her that was full of weird eddies and tiny whirlpools.

With the fresh offshore breeze hurrying them along, they made good progress and in something under an hour were drawing near to the steam yacht. Tony stared at her fixedly with a puzzled frown knitting his brow.

" I seem to have seen that yacht before," he said.

" Isn't she lovely!" said Jack, intent on the sweeping sheer and towering masts. Then his expression changed.

" I know her!" he almost shouted.

His cry mingled with Tony's, who at the same moment cried " I remember her."

They stared at one another. Recognition had come to both simultaneously. There could be no mistake. The strange yacht was none other than the vessel which had passed them in the gale and, ignoring their signals of distress, had steamed away and left them to their fate. That the gallant little *Spray* had survived the storm and had brought her young crew to safety was no mitigation of the callous behaviour of those in authority in the steam yacht. For all they knew— or cared—the little craft might have been overwhelmed directly they were out of sight.

" I should like to go aboard and tell the skipper what I think of him," said Jack fiercely.

To his surprise, his chum took his suggestion seriously.

" We jolly well will," he announced.

" Do you think we'd better?" asked Jack after a moment's pause.

" Why not? We won't start by being rude, but I should love to ask him why, when we signalled for assistance, he ignored us and went off and left us in the lurch."

It was indeed the same vessel. There was no mistaking the shape of the bridge, the placing of the deckhouses and the flaring, defiant bow. The features had been indelibly fixed in the boys' memories.

" I don't see anyone on deck," said Jack.

" Never mind," said Tony. " Some of the crew

are sure to be aboard. They would not all go ashore
and leave a big vessel like that unattended on an open
coast. Roll up the jib. I see the accommodation ladder
is down. We'll run alongside it."

Obediently Jack rolled up the headsail, and Tony,
at the tiller, manœuvred his little craft, measuring the
distance with his eye.

Running alongside a vessel riding head to wind is
much the same as picking up the mooring buoy.
Not having the motor running, it was impossible to
" go astern " to check the way, and Tony had to judge
his distance so that, running up head to wind with the
sails shaking, the *Spray* would come to a standstill
just abreast of the little square grating at the bottom
of the ladder. He judged it perfectly, and the little
yawl nosed quietly up alongside the stage so gently
that Jack had only to put out his hand and grasp the
stanchion to hold her in position.

Tony cast off the halliards and lowered the mainsail.
He looked up at the yacht's rail. No heads showed
above it, staring down at them. No one appeared to
have seen them. Certainly no one took any interest
in them. He stepped out on to the grating.

" Give me the painter," he said. " I'll make it fast."

" Shall I come?" suggested Jack.

Tony pursed his lips.

" Better wait," he said. " You stay aboard and keep
the *Spray* from bumping the side. The skipper might
get in a rage if we marked his paint. We mustn't give
him a chance to put us in the wrong."

He pushed the *Spray* away with his foot and watched her drop clear, then he turned to mount the ladder.

"Tony, why Master Tony, what are you doing here?"

The voice came in a hoarse whisper. Tony stopped dead and looked round in surprise. For a moment he saw no one and could not think where the voice was coming from; then, to his astonishment, he saw the face of young Sam Tonkin framed in an open port inside the ladder.

"Sam!" he cried. "Then you are not dead. Oh, I am so glad!"

"Hist!" whispered the young fisherman. "Speak quietly. How did you know I was here?"

"I didn't," said Tony. "It was just luck. This yacht passed us in the storm without stopping to help us and I meant to ask the captain why he did it. What are you doing here?" asked Tony, in his turn. "Are you all right?"

"My leg is healing nicely and is almost well now," replied Sam. "The bullet went right through without touching anything important. I was lucky. But I'm practically a prisoner. They only let me on deck sometimes when we're out at sea."

"A prisoner!" cried Tony in surprise. "Why, what ship is this?"

"Don't you know? But of course you don't. She belongs to the crowd who hired me to land the contraband. After the dust-up in the cave and Joe Rogers came back saying he'd caught your friend and then someone had laid him out with a whack on the head and he'd got away, there was an awful rumpus. You see, they knew the game was up and they'd have to flit before the police got them. They locked me in that little room at the bottom of the stairs and I thought they meant to leave me there, but in the end they brought me along, though one fellow wanted to do me in. Some of us got away in my boat and the others went away in the cars."

"Your boat was found anchored on the fishing ground. Joe Small towed her in."

"Did he?" said Sam. "I'm glad of that. I got one of the fellows to slip the hook over to save her going adrift. He's not a bad chap, that one. We came out in her to this craft. She was waiting in the fog and we all got aboard."

"Do you say you're a prisoner?"

"Yes, the door is locked."

A sudden idea struck Tony.

"Is the key in the lock on the outside?" he asked.

"Yes," replied the fisherman. "Here, where are you going? Come back. They'll catch you too."

His words fell on ears that were intentionally deaf. Tony slipped to the top of the ladder and cautiously looked round the deck. It was deserted. Though he could hear voices from forward, the speakers were evidently hidden by the deckhouse, the entrance to which was right opposite the accommodation ladder. Tony crossed the deck on tiptoe and peeped inside. The vestibule was deserted and he could see a stairway leading to the lower deck. Sam's prison must be at its foot.

He stood a moment listening. There was no sound near him, though distant sounds from forward told of life in other parts of the vessel and down in the bowels of the ship a shovel clanged on an iron floor.

His canvas shoes made no noise, but he held his breath as he slipped down the stairs, to find himself in a passageway with several doors opening off it. One had a key in the lock and, from its position, Tony guessed it was Sam's prison. He tiptoed to it and his hand was on the key when another door farther along the passage opened and a man stepped out. Luckily, the door opening outwards, Tony was shielded from view as the man hesitated with one foot on the threshold for a last word with someone inside.

Tony, heart in mouth, turned and ran back up the stairs, but at the top a noise on the deck outside brought him to a sudden halt. Someone was approaching the door. His retreat was cut off. He had no choice. With enemies before and behind, there was only one way. Quickly he slipped into what proved to be the saloon, which luckily was empty.

A long table ran down the centre, with a row of chairs on either side, screwed to the floor. A white cloth covered the table, evidently in preparation for a meal, and hung low almost to the ground. Without a second thought, he plunged below it and, with wildly beating heart, crouched in the slender shelter.

Footsteps descended the stairs and a man entered

the saloon and seated himself at a desk standing in a corner against the bulkhead. Tony was trapped. Then, to his horror, he heard the sound of the winch, indicating that the anchor was being hove up. A few moments later the vibration of the hull made it obvious that the propellers were working and the vessel was actually under way.

CHAPTER XVIII

Jack Carries the News to the Hall

Jack, busy fending the *Spray* off the side of the yacht as she dropped back to the end of her mooring rope, did not see Tony speaking to Sam through the porthole. By the time the little yawl had settled to lie quietly with her rope taut and Jack had time to look about, the gangway was empty and Tony had disappeared.

Jack sat down in the stern sheets and prepared to take things comfortably while waiting for his chum. He was almost level with the taffrail, the huge counter, with the name *Medusa* in big gold letters printed on it, towered high above him and the truck on the *Spray's* masthead barely topped the bulwarks. He looked at the rudder and sternpost going down until it merged in the green of the water, and thought he could distinguish the tips of two of the propeller blades.

" Well, I'm dashed! If the young bloke hasn't actually made his boat fast to the gangway," said a voice above.

" These amateur fishermen is a fair pest," said another. " Cast him adrift, mate."

For a moment Jack did not realize that he was

the person referred to, then, to his surprise, he saw a man run down the ladder, untie his mooring rope from the stanchion and with a cheery " Here y'are, sonny!" throw it overboard.

" Hi, hold on!" he cried, springing to his feet a moment too late. Under the pressure of the wind, the *Spray* began to drift astern.

" My friend is aboard the yacht. Where is he?" he shouted again.

" What do you say?"

A head appeared above the rail.

" Oh, come on. We can't stay here all day," said another voice testily.

The two men tailed on to the fall and hauled the accommodation ladder up clear of the water.

" Stop!" shouted Jack again in desperation. " My friend is aboard, I tell you."

At that moment a noisy clanking broke out from forward and a wisp of white steam spurted from the steam yacht's side and blew aft in a white cloud, so that, even if the men had troubled to listen to him, his words were drowned by the noise. By this time the *Spray* had drifted clear of the stern and was steadily driving out to sea. Jack looked anxiously for a sign of Tony, but the high bulwark hid anyone on deck unless he actually came to the rail. Save for an officer on the distant bridge, he could see no one.

Suddenly to his dismay he saw the water boil under the huge counter. The propeller was working and a rush of water swept towards him, twisting the *Spray* round in the swirling eddies. The steam yacht had hove up her anchor and was under way and Tony was still aboard.

Jack could scarcely believe his eyes. What had become of Tony? With a growing feeling of helplessness, he watched the big craft sweep round in a wide circle and head eastward along the coast. Standing in the stern sheets, he waited, expecting every minute to see her turn back towards him, but she held undeviatingly on her course, and at last he realized that he was indeed abandoned.

What should he do? Obviously the first thing to do was to get back to Barlash Cove and let Major Bamford know what had happened. Should he hoist the sails? By this time he had a very good idea how to handle them, but the wind was fresh and, without Tony to prompt him, he might make a mess of something. The motor was another matter. He felt confident that he could manage that; also, with the steady thrust of the propeller urging her on, the *Spray* would cover the distance more quickly.

His mind made up, he soon had the motor purring. He slipped in the clutch and the little craft, no longer drifting aimlessly, but under control once more, quickly gathered way and forged ahead. Taking the tiller, he opened the throttle wide and headed her back along the coast for Barlash Cove. The wind was abeam and presently he unrolled he jib, so that with two sails to help the motor the *Spray* slipped along at a good pace.

It was unfortunate that the steam yacht had gone off in the opposite direction, but that could not be helped. Tony threw many backward glances over his shoulder, hoping against hope to see her returning, but he was disappointed. She soon merged in the distant coastline and, save for a fishing boat or two and a large tramp steamer far out on the horizon, the sea was bare.

A little over an hour later he entered the cove and, it being high water, did not wait to pick up the moorings and row ashore in the dinghy, but ran straight alongside the boatbuilder's wharf.

" Where's Master Tony?" cried Mr. Pascoe, a note of anxiety in his voice. " Have you landed him somewhere? Don't say he's overboard."

His jaw dropped and his eyes opened wide when Jack told him, in as few words as possible, what had happened.

" The steam yacht that passed ye in the gale," he repeated, as though hardly able to credit his senses. " And you say young Master Tony went aboard her and she hove up anchor and steamed away without you setting eyes on him again? Well now, if that don't beat all. It's a main queer start, sure enough. What are ye going to do about it? You must let the Major know first thing."

" That's why I ran in alongside here, instead of going to moorings. I thought it would save time if you moored the *Spray* up for me. I'm going straight to the Hall."

" So it will, now, so it will. Don't you worry about the *Spray*. We'll see to her. Tom!" His voice rose to a stentorian bellow with such a note of urgency in it that not only his son but every workman in the yard came running out of the sheds to see what was wanted. " Look to the *Spray*, Tom, and you, young master, let the Major know just as soon as you can. I don't know what to think."

Jack needed no second bidding, but, leaving the worthy boatbuilder scratching his head in perplexity, set out for the Hall at his top speed, and was lucky enough to meet the Major giving the dogs a walk in the grounds.

" Hullo!" he cried cheerily, " you're in a hurry. Where's Tony?"

For the second time Jack told his story, giving more details than he had done to the boatbuilder. As he listened the Major's smile faded and his face grew stern.

" It was foolish, very foolish," he commented. " Tony should never have gone aboard. However, it's too late to think of that now. I simply cannot understand it. To kidnap a boy in that fashion. What can they mean to do? If it is simply a joke to give him a scare and they intend to land him somewhere, it is one I do not appreciate and if I can make them suffer for it I will. She went east, you say, and she has a good two hours' start. She may be many miles away by this time."

He stood for a moment in thought.

" I'm sorry I suggested it," said Jack miserably.

" That's all right, boy," said the Major kindly. " I don't blame you. Come," he added, setting off at a quick pace for the house.

Once in his study, the Major set the wires to work. First he got in touch with the Dovermouth police and reported the facts to them. That done, he rang up the coast guards and, by telephoning to the different stations along the coast, he at length got word that a vessel answering to the yacht's description was in sight about forty miles away steaming in an easterly direction.

" Forty miles," mused the Major, half to himself, but loud enough for Jack, who stood at his elbow, to hear. " She'll be passing Livermouth soon, where there may be a naval vessel or two. My old friend Bitterne is in command there. He might be able to help us."

Once more he picked up the receiver and in a few moments was in communication with his friend, Rear-Admiral Bitterne.

While his conversation was satisfactory in one sense, it was disquieting in another. Admiral Bitterne gave the Major the information in confidence that the steam yacht *Medusa* had come under suspicion on account of her peculiar habit of anchoring off the coast instead of entering port, and the authorities were wondering if she had anything to do with the drug smuggling which had been attracting their attention for some time.

No Admiralty vessel suitable for the job was in port and ready for sea, but an armed trawler, one of the fishery patrol boats which cruise along the coast to prevent foreigners from fishing in our territorial waters, was farther eastward, and the Admiral promised to get in touch with her by radio and tell her to stop the yacht and bring her into port.

" It is an excellent excuse to lay our hands on her. We have wanted a chance to overhaul her for long enough, but could not do so for lack of evidence."

" So far, so good," said Major Bamford, laying down the instrument. " We've done all we can. There's nothing left for us now but to wait—and waiting is often the worst part of all.

" We won't wait here at any rate," he said suddenly. " It's too trying. We'll go over to Livermouth in the car. We'll learn all the news there is to learn without delay. Come along."

Ten minutes later they were speeding along the roads at a good sixty miles an hour.

CHAPTER XIX

The Patrol Boat

Tony, crouching under the table in the *Medusa's* saloon, was a prey to varied emotions. Had he not had the conversation with Sam, he would, of course, have acted very differently and would at once have made his presence known.

His idea in getting below had been to unlock the door of Sam's cabin, when they would both have retreated to the *Spray* and so made their escape. This plan had been frustrated and now, by his action, he had put himself in a false position. It was too late to declare himself and, knowing the type of men he had to deal with, his only course was to wait in the hope that an opportunity of escape would present itself.

Slowly the minutes passed. Lunch time was drawing near and presently a steward came in and commenced to lay the table. Watching the man's feet passing hither and thither, Tony suddenly realized that his refuge could only be a temporary one, for the table was narrow and when the diners sat down there would be little space between their feet, and his presence was almost certain to be discovered.

From his lowly position, he took stock of his surroundings. The door by which he had entered was close to the writing table at which the man sat, so escape by it was out of the question. The sides of the saloon were flanked by long settees and the only other exit was a door at the after end.

Cautiously working his way along under the table, Tony waited until the steward had left the saloon, then crawled to the door and tried the handle, to reach which he had to stand up. Looking over his shoulder as he did so, he was horrified to see a mirror hanging above the desk in such a position that the man had only to glance up into it to see him.

For a moment he stood stock still as though petrified, his heart beating painfully in his breast, but, luckily, the man had paused and, chin cupped in hand, had his head turned to stare idly out of a port. With an effort, Tony recovered his wits. He turned the handle, the door opened, and, without a thought as to what might be on the other side, he slipped through, pulling the door to behind him as noiselessly as he could.

His luck held. He found himself in a small cloak-room, containing a wash basin and a row of hooks from which a number of oilskin and other coats were suspended. Besides the one by which he had entered, there were two other doors. One gave access to an inner compartment and the second, which was hooked a few inches ajar, he found, to his relief, led out on deck.

His relief was short-lived. As he approached the

door, he heard voices outside and, through the crack, saw two men walking towards him. He looked wildly round for a hiding-place, and in desperation slipped behind the coats, but, instead of entering, the men swung about and tramped aft. Tony breathed a sigh of relief once more as he realized that they were taking " a constitutional ", getting exercise by " walking the quarter deck ".

But though they had not discovered him, their presence had effectually cut off his retreat. Still standing half hidden by the oilskins, Tony rapidly weighed his chances. At any moment now the lunch bell might ring. If he could remain hidden till then, the three men, and any others that might be aboard, would congregate in the saloon. The crew also might have their meal at the same time. In that case, save for the helmsman and the officer on the bridge and possibly, though hardly probably in a vessel of that size and such clear weather, a lookout forward, the decks would be deserted and he would have a chance to find a more permanent refuge where he might hide until some port was reached, when, perhaps under cover of the friendly darkness, he might slip ashore and even yet release Sam. Going into the inner compartment, he bolted the door and waited.

He had not long to wait. A bell rang and he heard the two men pass through the cloak-room and settle in their places at table, then the desultory hum of conversation and the tinkle of crockery sounded through the bulkhead.

Now was his chance. The stern of the vessel was deserted, as he had expected. Quickly he stepped out on deck. He peeped cautiously round the corner of the deckhouse. The stretch of white deck was untenanted. Forward of the deckhouse he could see the engine-room skylight, then the fiddley and the massive yellow funnel, while, beyond again, stretching across the ship from side to side, with a smaller deckhouse below it, was the bridge, on which a man in uniform was pacing back and forth.

Having taken this in, Tony slipped across to peep round the other corner, where a similar sight met his gaze.

Backwards and forwards paced the officer, from one end of the bridge to the other, with occasional pauses to stare ahead, or at some distant object which caught his attention.

Watching until the officer had passed out of sight, Tony darted forward, stooping below the level of the portholes and keeping close to the deckhouse so as to be unseen by the people inside. He reached the shelter of the engine-room skylight just as the officer recrossed into view. The skylight was open and the hot air, redolent of oil, swept out and over him in waves of sickly heat.

Resisting the impulse to peep down at the whirling masses of gleaming metal, which kept up a rhythmic song, Tony looked round for a hiding-place.

A motor launch in davits, resting on skids above the rail, caught his eye. It was well above the deck and almost on a level with the bridge, so that, if he could climb into it and crouch down, he would be completely out of sight and safe from discovery unless someone climbed up and actually looked into the boat —a most unlikely contingency at that time of day, for most of the cleaning aboard a yacht is done in the forenoon. Such a position would have a further advantage, as from there he would command a wide view and would know exactly what was going on—a thing that would be impossible if he hid away in some cupboard or empty cabin below.

The officer ceased his pacing and stood staring stolidly ahead. Tony watched him with a growing impatience. Should he risk it? He noted where he would place his feet and the hand-holds necessary for him to climb swiftly into the boat. As he braced himself for the effort, the officer turned, stared aft for a few moments, scanning the sea astern, and then, to Tony's relief, resumed his measured " sentry go ".

Tony watched his chance. As the officer disappeared behind the chart-house, he made his attempt. Two quick strides and a lithe bound, and he was on the rail; grasping the gunwale, he swung himself up and a moment later rolled into the bottom of the boat, where he lay panting, not so much from the exertion as from excitement.

He now felt comparatively safe and had time to think of things other than the risk of immediate discovery. He found it a not too cheery occupation. While he knew enough about his unsuspecting hosts to wish to keep clear of them at all costs, there were many things he did not know and he wondered what would be the outcome of his rash venture. What had become of Jack and the *Spray*? Except that she was no longer alongside, he had no idea. Miles astern he could see a speck on the water which might be his little craft, but it was too far away to be certain. Almost an hour had passed since the yacht got under way and, though she appeared to be steaming in a leisurely fashion, slipping through the water with little fuss, she must have covered a distance of about ten miles. To port the coast slid steadily past. It was strange to him, for, by sea, he had never been farther east than Dovermouth.

Presently the meal in the saloon came to an end and the three men, with a fourth, who by his dress appeared to be the captain, came out on deck. The sight of them reminded Tony that he was both hungry and thirsty, for he had had nothing since his breakfast. But there was no help for that. He must " tighten his belt " and bear it. The men stood talking for a time just below his refuge and then moved away.

All afternoon the *Medusa* kept on her leisurely way. Had Tony only known it, the cruise was simply killing time until darkness would enable to be put into operation a scheme which the miscreants wished to carry out; for, though foiled at Barlash, they were part of a big organization and must make other arrangements for landing their " goods ".

About five o'clock, as far as Tony could tell—for

he had forgotten to wind his wrist watch, and the old sea custom of striking " the bells " every half-hour was not kept up aboard the yacht—he became aware of a growing excitement on deck.

When he sat up he could see the people on the bridge, and now the officer on watch had been joined by the captain and the three men. From their behaviour and the way they stared seaward, it was obvious that something was causing them uneasiness. What could it be?

Reconnoitring the deck to make sure that it was deserted, Tony knelt up, taking care to keep the davit falls between himself and the group on the bridge. At first he could see nothing, for his view was curtailed by the funnel and superstructure, but presently, some distance away, he saw what at first sight he took to be a smart grey-painted trawler, steaming on a course which converged with their own. Even as he watched, a string of flags fluttered aloft from her wheelhouse and then he recognized the white ensign of his Majesty's fleet fluttering from the flagstaff aft. With a thrill of joy he realized that it was one of the fishery protection cruisers and that she wished to communicate with the yacht.

Now what would the villains do?

Tony could not read the flags, but it was evident that the men on the bridge knew their meaning. The telegraph bell clanged and Tony waited expectantly to hear the engines slow down, but after a few moments he realized, to his surprise, that it was not an order to stop that had been signalled to the engineer, but one for increased speed. The *Medusa* responded, and the swish and swirl of the water alongside grew louder.

The patrol boat kept her signal flying and, getting no answer, drew attention to it by a blast on her whistle.

Still the *Medusa* held on her way. Sounds indicative of increased effort came from below. A boiler door clanged and shovels scraped and clattered on the plates of the stokehold floor. Presently a cloud of smoke issued from the funnel.

The captain of the patrol boat was not slow to note these signs. Her slim grey funnel belched smoke in its turn as she responded to the challenge, while her course was altered slightly to cut the yacht off.

Hardly able to restrain his excitement, Tony was in danger of betraying his presence in his anxiety to see what was going on, but, luckily for him, the crew of the *Medusa* were as interested as he and had eyes for little else but their job and their pursuer.

Presently two of the men came down from the bridge and went below, to reappear a little later carrying a number of tin canisters. They made a second journey and then a third, till the canisters became quite a heap. Then they fetched several stout canvas bags and stowed the canisters inside, after which they roped the bags together, attached two pieces of iron ballast as sinkers and dropped the lot overboard, leaving a thin line with a ring of corks, such as fishermen use, to mark the spot, so that they would be able to recover them again. All this was done on Tony's side of the deck, so that their movements were hidden from the patrol boat by the deckhouses.

Tony, keeping carefully out of sight, watched the proceedings with interest. He realized that incriminating evidence of some sort was being got rid of in case they were captured. Looking shoreward, he mentally noted certain " marks " on the coast—a small farmhouse in line with a distant hill-top—which would enable him to find the buoy again.

For a time the patrol boat held her position, then, as the pressure of steam in the *Medusa's* boilers gradually increased, Tony realized, with a spasm of dismay, that she was slowly but none the less surely losing ground. A few minutes more and it was plain beyond all doubt that in point of speed the yacht could show her heels to the Government craft.

A prey to disappointment, Tony sank down on the bottom-boards and stared unseeingly at the motor. Oh, if only he could disable the *Medusa* in some way! Bring her to a standstill, or even reduce her speed and give the patrol boat time to come up with her. The engines! But what could he do to them? Besides, the engineers were on the alert and would not fail to see him. The anchors! Could he let go an anchor? They were not far from the coast, so the water was not likely to be so deep that it would not reach the bottom. In any case, an anchor and chain dragging through the water would slow the vessel up. That might be sufficient.

Tony did not know how an anchor in a vessel as large as the *Medusa* was secured, or if it was possible for him to let it go unaided, but he might be able to do it. It was worth trying, anyway.

In the after locker of the launch, Tony had noticed a khaki-coloured overall suit, evidently belonging to one of the crew. Probably the man who had charge of the launch kept it there and slipped it on when he worked the motor. In the hope that it might serve as a disguise, Tony put it on. It was much too large for him, but, by turning up the sleeves and legs, he made it a passable fit.

Thus camouflaged, Tony peeped over the side of the launch and reconnoitred forward and aft. His side of the ship was entirely deserted. Such of the crew as could leave their posts were congregated on the opposite side, intent on their pursuer. He dropped to the deck and, running lightly forward, stopped under the bridge, where he was safe from observation by those above.

Forward of the bridge there was little cover. Save for a couple of comparatively low skylights, the deck was bare until the curving forehatch was reached. Several of the crew stood in a group by the bulwarks on the starboard side, just aft of the foremast rigging. The port side was clear, but any advance from his present refuge and he would be in the open and in full view, not only of the crew but of those on the bridge above.

Tony hesitated, then, setting his teeth, made up

his mind. To rush it was useless. Such an action would merely draw attention to himself. He must trust to his disguise and the fact that no one was likely to pay much attention to him.

At as quick a pace as he dared, he walked forward. With every step he expected to hear the challenging shout that would herald his discovery, but none came. Never before had Tony so appreciated the old saying that " Fortune favours the brave ". He passed un-noticed behind the group of sailors, not one of whom even turned his head, and, if any on the bridge saw him, they mistook him, as he had hoped they might, for one of the crew going to the forecastle on some errand.

At the forehatch he paused for a quick glance round. No one was looking his way. Even the helmsman was craning his neck forward to get a look at the patrol boat, on whose deck some half a dozen blue-jackets were congregated round the long-barrelled, slender gun. Wasting no time, Tony slipped behind the forehatch and, scarcely able to believe in his good fortune, crouched down behind it, shielded from view.

The cables and the huge winch were now before him. The first sight of the latter was rather dis-heartening, but after a while he felt a growing con-fidence. About two years before, his father and he had been invited to spend a few days cruising in a small steam yacht. Her kindly skipper had taken Tony under his wing and, amongst other things, had explained her winch to him. He had forgotten the details, but, now that he had what appeared to be its big brother before him, the working of the mechanism came back to him.

He studied the giant carefully. Yes, that would be the handle that cleared the chain wheel, giving it the " free wheel " action, and that other would lift the brake and release the chain.

He hoped he was right. How he hoped he was right! In any case, it was no use waiting. He peeped round the corner. No one was looking his way.

Heart in mouth, he stepped forward. A few seconds of frenzied work and with a heavy splash the huge stockless anchor fell from the hawsepipe into the sea. At the same moment a dull boom sounded across the water. The patrol boat had fired her gun.

The rattle and roar of the cable running out, as the anchor plunged below, filled the crew of the *Medusa* with dismay. As Tony had surmised, the sea was not deep. The anchor reached the sea bed, gripping and tearing away time after time. The *Medusa* quivered in a series of terrific vibrations, the deck seemed to bend underfoot, and all, even those on the bridge, found themselves indulging in an involuntary but none the less vigorous " step dance ".

The captain staggered across the bridge to the engine-room telegraph and wrenched the handle to " Stop ". As he did so there was a jarring crack. The *Medusa* snubbed violently and, as the rattle of flying chain was drowned in the tearing roar of rending metal, a cloud of sparks burst from under the bows. Then the noise suddenly ceased and the vibrating of the hull gradually subsided.

The boatswain, who during the sudden pandemonium had " danced " helplessly with the rest, rushed forward to peer over the bows.

" The starboard anchor and cable have gone, sir!" he shouted to the captain on the bridge. " The hawsepipe has burst and we are cut down to below the waterline."

Consternation reigned. The anchor, let go when the vessel was steaming at full speed, had gripped the sea bed. The terrific strain had proved too much for the hawsepipe and, once that had gone, the chain had cut through the comparatively thin plating of the hull like so much butter. The forepeak was already full of water. The *Medusa* was " down by the head " and only the collision bulkhead kept her from filling altogether. With her bow sunk as though she hung her head in shame, she must humbly wait and surrender to her pursuer.

CHAPTER XX

A Bluff that Failed

While the crew's attention was distracted by the commotion, Tony had not been idle. His work accomplished, he ran aft. If anyone saw him, they took no notice, probably thinking he was one of the crew who, frightened out of his wits, was racing out of danger. In a few moments he was safely ensconced behind a heavy curtain in the deckhouse under the bridge. Barely was he in hiding when the three men entered.

" We must get rid of that young fisherman," the short, stout man, who seemed to be the leader, was saying. " If they found him, he might talk. For the rest, I think we can bluff it out."

" Right, boss," said the second man. " Tom. You've got your gun. Fetch him up."

" You'd better both go. We don't want any blood. It might take some explaining. A knock on the head should quieten him and, if he isn't dead, he soon will be if you slip him over with a couple of firebars on his feet as sinkers. There'll be nothing to give the show away then."

" All right. Only let's get on with it," said

Tom. "That patrol boat'll be up in five minutes."

"There's plenty of time," said the third man. "It'll take them another ten minutes to launch a boat and row her over here. We can do our little job behind the deckhouse. They won't see through that."

"That's right," the "boss" agreed. "Only don't waste time and don't bungle it. I should get the sinkers here first. There's no use in telling the crew more than they need know."

As the two men left the cabin, the "boss" moved to a port and stood looking out at the approaching patrol boat, which was still some distance away. Tony, scarcely daring to breathe, had listened to this cold-blooded plot to murder young Sam Tonkin, with a growing anger and dismay. He had no doubt but that he would share the same fate were he discovered. Doubtless he might remain in hiding until the boarding party from the patrol boat arrived, when he could reveal himself with safety, and his testimony would bring the villains to justice, but that would be poor comfort if Sam were murdered in the meantime.

No. If Sam were to be saved, there was no time to lose. It was a risk and a big one, but he must act and act quickly. Quietly he slipped from behind the curtain, hoping to reach the door unseen, but luck, which for so long had favoured him, now passed him by. The "boss" turned and saw him.

"Hullo!" he said. "What are you doing here?" Then his expression changed. "Who are you?" he demanded.

With a threatening gesture, he approached the boy. Tony backed away. The man was not much taller than himself and did not look in the best of condition, but he was much heavier, and in a rough and tumble weight tells, while at any moment the others might return.

"Come here," roared the "boss" in a sudden burst of rage. He lunged forward. Tony slid round the corner of the table to avoid him. The "boss" followed. Round and round they went, once, twice, a third time. The pace was hot. Tony heard his antagonist's breath coming in great gasps. As he had suspected, he was out of condition. One more round and he let his foe gain a little. The "boss's" arm reached out for the elusive collar of Tony's coat.

Suddenly Tony changed his tactics. Turning, he seized the outstretched arm by the wrist with both hands, twisted to one side, drew the arm over his shoulder and lunged forward in two or three quick steps, bending half double and drawing the arm downwards in front of him as he did so.

It was the old wrestler's trick, "the flying mare". Old Sam, who had been a noted wrestler in the West Country in his youth, had shown him how to do it, but it is a "heavy" throw and liable to be dangerous if badly done, so Tony had never experimented with it on any of his friends. Now, in his desperate strait, he tried it and was surprised to find it so easy.

Taken completely by surprise, the "boss", heavy as he was, found himself sailing helplessly over Tony's head, to fall with a terrific crash in the corner. He squirmed for a moment and then, with a groan, lay still.

Tony wasted no time on his vanquished opponent, for he knew there was none to spare. Already he heard footsteps approaching the open door on the starboard side, so he slipped out of the opposite door and ran aft. He met no one and gained the main deckhouse unmolested. It was empty. Quickly he slipped down the stairs and made straight for Sam's cabin.

Yes. The key was still in the lock. Sam was staring out of a porthole at the approaching patrol boat, but he turned at the sound of the opening door.

" Hullo, Tony," he burst out. " Whatever——"

" Hush!" whispered Tony breathlessly. " Don't say a word, but come out."

" Why——"

" Oh, please be quick. They mean to murder you."

Sam needed to hear no more. He was out in the passage in a moment. Tony pulled the door to and, locking it, pocketed the key.

" That should bother them a bit," he said.

Suddenly they heard voices.

" What's that you say? The ' boss ' knocked out? Who by?"

" Oh, he's half-dazed yet. He says there's a strange boy aboard and he had a scrap with him, but I reckon it was more than a boy that fixed him like he is. We're to search the ship. Got your gun?"

" Sure."

"Come on, then. On deck and be quick. Them blame sailors'll be aboard nosing round directly."

The boys breathed again. They could count on a short respite.

"Hold on," said the first voice again. "What about that fisherman fellow?"

"Leave him alone. We know where he is. We can get him when we want him. We must find the other first."

In spite of their danger, the boys grinned at each other.

"I know," whispered Sam. "Follow me."

Tiptoeing up the stairs, they peeped out of a port. The searchers were working aft, one on each side of the deck, and one of them, setting a foot on a projection, stood up to see that no one was hiding on the top of the deckhouse. There was no one else about, for the crew were at work forward shoring up the collision bulkhead, which alone prevented the yacht from filling and sinking like a stone.

"Quick!" whispered Sam, as the men disappeared aft.

Leaping up, he caught the lintel of the door and swung himself up on to the top of the deckhouse. It was an agile feat, requiring considerable strength, and Tony watched in dismay, knowing that it was impossible for him to imitate it, but, lying flat, Sam extended a hand, and a moment later Tony found himself hoisted up beside his friend.

"Into the middle and lie flat," whispered Sam.

" You face forward and I'll face aft, and then we can't be taken by surprise."

" What about the bridge? Anyone could see us from the end."

" I don't believe anybody is up there. Anyway, we must chance that."

From their hiding-place, they heard the men search the saloon and eventually go below. The patrol boat was now close by. She stopped and lowered a boat, which, with four men and an officer in it, rowed over to the yacht.

The captain with the " boss ", who had a large purple lump showing through his scanty hair, stood at the head of the gangway.

" We can't find the boy, and that fisherman fellow has got out of his cabin."

Tony and Sam heard the whispered report as the boat drew near.

" What?" The " boss's " jaw dropped. " Are they on deck?"

" No. I'm sure of that. They're hiding below some-where."

" Then keep them below at all costs. With luck, I'll bluff this out. When we get clear we can settle with them."

The officer, pistol holster strapped to his waist, climbed aboard, followed by three armed seamen.

" I protest against this outrage, sir," said the " boss ", stepping forward. " To fire a shot at an unarmed yacht."

"A blank shot. You should have stopped," responded the officer.

"Blank," cried the "boss" indignantly. "It blew a hole in my bow and knocked my anchor away. We're in danger of sinking, sir."

"I notice you are badly down by the head, but our shot was blank for all that," said the officer coolly, though with a slightly puzzled look on his face.

"But see the damage for yourself. You must have fired a shot. How else do you account for it?"

Tony was unable to restrain himself any longer. He scrambled to his feet.

"Because I let go the anchor," he cried.

Had the patrol boat actually fired a shell, it could not have caused greater surprise. The "boss" turned livid with rage, and the captain smothered a curse.

"That boy stowed away in this ship," said the "boss", who evidently had difficulty in restraining his fury. "He assaulted me. I know nothing of him. Take him into custody."

"I'm not a policeman," snapped the officer, shortly. "Who are you?" he demanded of Tony.

"My name is Tony Bamford, sir," replied Tony. "They're armed, sir. Be careful. They meant to murder me."

The "boss" must have realized that the game was lost, but, desperately, he played his last card.

"Murder him! Ridiculous! The boy must be mad. Why, until a few minutes ago I did not even know he was on board. Now, sir, is this farce to end?"

" He did, sir, really," cried Tony. " And they meant to murder Sam too. Here's Sam," he added, pulling the young fisherman, who grinned somewhat sheepishly, to his feet. " They were going to throw his body overboard with weights on it, but I let him out of the cabin where he was locked up, and we hid until you came. They'd have dropped him over on the other side where you could not have seen them, like they did with a lot of cases when you first started to chase us. There's a buoy on the end of a line like a fisherman's crab-pot mark, so you'll be able to find them easily enough and see if I speak the truth."

To say that this little speech, fired off at top speed, caused consternation is to put it mildly.

" You are under arrest," said the officer, sharply, to the " boss ". " Search them for arms."

One by one, beginning with the " boss ", the search was carried out, and resulted in half a dozen automatic pistols being discovered. The sailors, under command of the mate of the yacht, were ordered to carry on with their job, but the " boss ", the captain and the other two civilians were ferried over to the patrol boat and kept under guard, while, in answer to a wireless message, tugs came out to assist the damaged vessel into port.

Tony and Sam also transferred to the patrol boat, and Tony learned how Jack and the *Spray* had fared, and how Jack's message had been instrumental in sending the " little man-of-war " to his aid.

·   ·   ·   ·   ·   ·   ·   ·   ·

There is little more to tell. The " boss " proved, indeed, to be the boss of a big organization of dope smugglers who had been troubling the authorities with their activities for a long time. Tony and Jack were called as witnesses at his trial, which resulted in his being put in a place where he could do no more harm for several years to come. The boys were complimented by the judge for the assistance they had given in bringing a scoundrel to justice. Indeed, they got " into the news ", and an enterprising press photographer visited Barlash and took their photographs aboard the *Spray*, so that they found themselves almost famous.

Poor Sam! He had not realized the wrong that he had been helping to do. He was allowed to turn king's evidence, which, knowing how his late *confrères* meant to treat him, he did not consider a " sneaky " thing to do, and his depositions helped the authorities very considerably. He returned to Barlash a rather chastened young man.

" You are well out of it, Sam," said the Major when, with the boys, he chanced to meet him in the village.

" I reckon I am, sir, thanks to Master Tony," replied Sam, with a grin at his friend. " Easy money's all right, but from now on the fishing'll be good enough for me."

" Yes," agreed the Major. " Honesty is still the best policy, after all."

" You're right," said Sam heartily.